Mills & Boon
Best Seller Romance

A chance to read and collect some of the best-loved novels from Mills & Boon—the world's largest publisher of romantic fiction.

Every month, four titles by favourite Mills & Boon authors will be re-published in the *Best Seller Romance* series.

A list of other titles in the *Best Seller Romance* series can be found at the end of this book.

Anne Mather

FORBIDDEN

MILLS & BOON LIMITED
LONDON · TORONTO

All the characters in this book have no existence outside the imagination of the Author, and have no relation whatsoever to anyone bearing the same name or names. They are not even distantly inspired by any individual known or unknown to the Author, and all the incidents are pure invention.

The text of this publication or any part thereof may not be reproduced or transmitted in any form or by any means, electronic or mechanical, including photocopying, recording, storage in an information retrieval system, or otherwise, without the written permission of the publisher.

This book is sold subject to the condition that it shall not, by way of trade or otherwise, be lent, resold, hired out or otherwise circulated without the prior consent of the publisher in any form of binding or cover other than that in which it is published and without a similar condition including this condition being imposed on the subsequent purchaser.

First published 1976
Australian copyright 1982
Philippine copyright 1982
This edition 1982

© *Anne Mather 1976*

ISBN 0 263 73986 4

Set in Linotype Baskerville 10 on 11 pt
02-0882

Made and printed in Great Britain by Richard Clay (The Chaucer Press) Ltd, Bungay, Suffolk

CHAPTER ONE

THE temperature of the pool was about eight degrees, the way he liked it. He swam several lengths swiftly, enjoying the sudden cooling of his flesh after the heat of his bed, and then climbed out to drip water on to the delicately coloured mosaic-tiled surround. Overnight winds had swept a few leaves on to the pool's surface, but he still preferred it to the clinically clean depths of the heated indoor pool which Deborah favoured. He towelled himself dry and as he did so his eyes flickered cynically over the ornate wrought iron and statuary which gave the pool area such an elegant background. It was a curious paradox, he thought, pulling on a navy towelling robe, that Deborah, who despised the naked human form in the flesh, should find such pleasure in looking at these stone images in all their flaunting detail.

Beyond the wrought iron trelliswork, presently hung with roses, a belt of poplar and cypress shielded the pool from prying eyes, and beyond that the tall walls surrounding the grounds assured absolute privacy. At this hour of the morning, no one else was abroad, however, and he walked back to the house deep in thought.

Shallow steps led up to a wide terrace, and he entered the house through french doors into a wide, high-ceilinged lounge. His bare feet left dusty imprints upon the cushion-soft thickness of the cream carpet, and his towel swung dangerously near an exquisite figurine, sculpted out of ivory, which occupied a central position on a low antique carved table. But he was unaware of it, absorbed as he was with the problems on his mind. He scarcely acknowledged the polite greeting addressed to him by Mrs. French, the housekeeper, who was drawing back the long silk curtains from the hall windows, and ascended the stairs two at a time to reach his own suite of rooms.

He showered in the brown and gold luxury of his bathroom and then dressed in the dark brown pin-striped suit he would wear to the office. He was fastening the laces of his suede boots when there was a tap at his bedroom door.

'Yes?'

His summons was unnecessarily brusque, but his lean features softened when a girl of perhaps sixteen came into the room. She was thin and dark, as he was, but without his height, and their relationship was at once apparent.

'Daddy,' she exclaimed appealingly, coming into the room and closing the door, 'I have to talk to you.' She leaned back against the door. 'Please – don't let Mummy do this!'

'Laura, we've been through all this—'

'I know, I know. But you could make her change her mind, I know you could.'

Her father came towards her, his expression compassionate, but firm. 'It happens that I don't want to change your mother's mind,' he told her gently. 'Laura, you're too young—'

'Oh – *stuff*!' The girl's lips trembled. 'Daddy, you don't understand!'

'I wonder how many other parents have been told that.'

'Well, it's true! You don't. You don't know what it's like to be in love—'

'Don't I?' Her father's lips tightened. 'I married your mother,' he reminded her quietly. 'We had you.'

'But you were never in love with her, were you?' Laura's eyes were stormy. 'I know you weren't. You were just two people from the same class in society who happened to suit one another at the time!'

'That's enough, Laura!'

'No, it isn't. It's not nearly enough. If you'd ever loved somebody, really loved them, that is, you'd have a little idea how I feel.'

'Laura, believe me, I know how you feel,' he answered

curtly, turning away, feeling a long-suppressed emotion stirring inside him. 'But I have no more time to argue with you. I have a meeting at ten—'

'Meetings, meetings! That's all you ever think about, isn't it? Work, work, work! You don't care about me any more than Mummy does. I'm just a puppet to be pulled about in whatever direction suits you best!'

'Laura!' He turned to face her again, and she wilted a little under the coldness of his gaze. 'The matter is closed, do you understand?'

'I – I'll be the laughing stock of my friends,' she persisted tremulously. 'H – having a governess at my age!'

'I don't see why. You've been ill. You can tell them that the doctor has recommended that you don't return to Boscombe for the time being. Then later ...' He shrugged. 'You're not exactly being confined to the house, you know.'

'I might as well be. All my friends will be away.'

'Only in term time. And besides, you're sixteen. Old enough to have grown out of the need for group relationships.'

'But not old enough to have a boy-friend?'

'Not that particular – boy-friend, at any rate.'

'Why not? Just because Johnny's ten years older than me and has to work for his living! Physically work, that is. Mummy doesn't really care about that, you know. She's only jealous—'

'Laura, be silent! We will not discuss this any further, do you hear? I suggest you go and get dressed and try to behave like the maturing female creature you're purporting to be.'

'But, Daddy—'

Laura made one final attempt to appeal to him, but one look at his grim controlled face was sufficient to convince her that she was wasting her time, and what was more, losing the only ally she was likely to have.

Later, as he was absentmindedly eating his breakfast in

the sun-filled morning room while he studied the *Financial Times*, he heard the squeal of Deborah's wheelchair coming across the hall. His wife had her suite of rooms on the ground floor for obvious reasons, and she rarely joined him for breakfast. In fact, Deborah rarely rose before he left, and he could only assume Laura had been foolish enough to disturb her mother. He put his paper aside and rose to his feet as the electric chair came into the room.

If one could discount the useless lower limbs always hidden beneath trousers or ankle-length skirts, Deborah Booth looked still a beautiful woman, even though she was confined to a wheelchair, and had been so for the past sixteen years. In her youth, she had loved horses and hunting better than anything, or anyone, and in spite of her husband's opposition had gone riding only weeks before her baby was due to be born. The fall she had had had almost killed the premature child and had crippled Deborah for life. In the beginning, she had blamed her husband for the accident, and for weeks she had refused to see either him or their small daughter. She had never wanted children and she had convinced herself that her pregnancy had been responsible for that momentary lack of control. Later, however, as the full implications of her incapacity were made known to her, she had had to acknowledge that she needed her husband now as never before. With a characteristic disregard for anyone's feelings but her own, she had insisted she could no longer live on the estate in Sussex which her father-in-law had given them as a wedding gift. Instead, they had moved to a house nearer London without the facilities for horses. She had demanded that all the animals be destroyed, and although James had not worshipped them as she had done, he missed the occasional opportunity to go riding. From his own point of view, he was nearer his work in the City, and this was a constant compensation; and apart from one occasion he had succeeded very well in adjusting to the often lonely tenor of his existence.

'Good morning, Deborah,' he said now, putting aside his table napkin. 'This is an unexpected – surprise.'

Deborah was still wearing her nightgown, a chiffon négligé accentuating her extreme thinness. 'What time will you be home this evening, James?' she inquired, without preamble.

He shrugged. 'Why do you ask? I have a provisional engagement for dinner with Tom Saunders, but it's nothing that can't wait if you've made other arrangements.'

'I see.' Deborah regarded him intently. 'Then I'd like you to come home to dinner. After all, the – er – governess arrives today, as you know, and I'd like you to be here to welcome her.' She paused, as though assessing his reactions. 'We may have trouble with Laura, and I'd prefer your – support.'

James accepted this without comment. It was a long time since Deborah had acknowledged needing his support in anything, but perhaps she was right on this occasion. Laura was inclined to be rebellious at times, and after his own conversation with her earlier ... Besides, Deborah did have a look of strain about her. He wondered if her back was paining her as it sometimes did. But she would not welcome *his* concern.

'All right,' he agreed equably. 'I'll be home around six.'

'Good.' Deborah smiled then, and the look of strain dispersed. 'It should be quite a – an interesting experiment.'

'Hardly an experiment,' remarked James dryly. 'I thought we had agreed it was the only solution.'

'Oh, it is, it is,' she hastened to reassure him. 'But I think it will be interesting all the same.'

James flicked back his cuff, consulting the plain gold watch encircling his wrist. 'It's after nine. I have to go, Deborah. I'll see you this evening.'

'Of course.'

Deborah nodded and he bent to kiss her cheek, aware of the way she flinched from his lips. Since her accident, he had never been allowed to lay a hand on her. The doctors had told him it was natural that she should feel this way in the beginning, paralysed as she was, but instead of the feeling diminishing over the years, it appeared to have increased. Not that he objected. In truth, such feeling as he had had for Deborah had died when he had been told how carelessly she had risked the life of their unborn child. But he was also aware that while Deborah might abhor his touch, she could become violently jealous if he showed any interest in other women.

It took him approximately fifty minutes to drive the thirty-three miles to his office near the Embankment. On motorways, the Jensen could have accomplished that distance in less than half the time, but James had grown accustomed to tempering its power to suit the conditions. The Booth Building had its own private parking area, and he left the Jensen in the capable hands of Charles, the commissionaire, before taking a lift to the penthouse floor. He entered his secretary's office just after ten, and Mrs. Sully gave him her usual cheerful smile.

'Good morning, Mr James,' she greeted him pleasantly. 'Your father has been ringing for you for the past fifteen minutes.'

'Has he?' James didn't sound perturbed as he crossed the outer office to his own sanctum with lithe indolent strides. 'What does he want?'

'I don't think he's very happy with those figures from Dryburn,' she replied reluctantly.

'Nor am I,' returned James dryly, opening his office door. 'Give me five minutes and then call him for me. Oh, and is there any coffee going begging?'

'I think your father expects you to go along to his office, Mr. James,' Mrs. Sully put in awkwardly, and James lifted a mocking eyebrow.

'You only think so? I *know* it, Mrs. Sully. But it won't

be the first time my father's had to delay blowing his gasket.'

The office beyond the dark wood-panelled door was wide and spacious. Two walls provided a generous amount of window area, presently filtering sunshine through the slats of the blinds, there were comfortable leather chairs, a leather-topped desk literally overflowing with files and papers, wire trays and other paraphernalia, and a plain honey-coloured carpet on the floor. This had been his father's office in the days when his grandfather had run their group of companies which traded under the name of Booth Industries, but since then there had been more expansion and although his father now controlled the group, it was no longer the limited family concern it had been. Now there were shareholders, and their position on the Stock Exchange to consider, and his father was increasingly shifting the burden of responsibility on to him.

When the call from his father's office came through, Robert Booth sounded angrily explosive. 'Where the hell have you been until this time of a morning?' he demanded, and then, without giving James time to reply, went on: 'I want you in this office in five minutes.'

'Calm down,' exclaimed James tolerantly, used to his father's uncertain temper. 'If it's the Dryburn figures that are bothering you, five minutes more or less are not going to make a lot of difference.'

'I'll say it's the Dryburn figures!' retorted his father. 'For heaven's sake, James, I sent you out to Hong Kong because I suspected Dryburn wasn't pulling his weight. But you didn't put any of this in your report, did you?'

'Not that Dryburn wasn't pulling his weight, no.'

'Stop playing with words, James. The man was idling his time and you didn't even notice! What in hell do you think I pay you for?'

'Dryburn was not idling his time,' remarked James coolly.

'How can you say that?'

'If you'll give me a chance to explain...'

'Huh!' His father snorted, but some of the fire had gone out of him. There was a moment's silence, and then he said: 'All right, all right. But it had better be good.'

'It is. Five minutes more, and I'll join you.'

James heard his father slam down his receiver at the other end of the line, and replaced his own with less emphasis. Perhaps he should have told the old man when he got back two weeks ago, but he had known the upheaval the truth would cause. Booth Industries being involved, even indirectly, with a giant drug-smuggling syndicate was sufficient to give his father apoplexy, and Robert Booth's blood pressure was a concern to them all. Still, the matter was in the hands of the police, and no doubt Sam Dryburn's name would soon be erased from the payroll of Booth Industries.

Fortunately, his father took the news of Dryburn's double-dealing rather better than James had expected. No doubt the realization that the figures were not a real reflection of the state of the company operating in Hong Kong was responsible for the softening of his manner, James thought cynically. In any event, Robert seemed anxious to bring their conversation round to more personal matters, and in his usual blunt way, he asked: 'How long does Deborah expect Laura to knuckle under to this kind of treatment?'

James decided he would have preferred discussing Dryburn's figures to this kind of interrogation, but with a shrug, he replied: 'I happen to agree with her, in this instance. Laura is too young to get involved with some Irish bricklayer.'

'Oh, I agree with you there,' his father assured him. 'Johnny Mooney is no suitable friend for her. But that's not the point, is it? Keeping the child at home, tutoring her in private, never allowing her the chance to see things for herself – that's not going to solve anything.'

'Would you have had us send her back to Boscombe?'
'Yes. Yes, I would.'
'And Mooney?'
'Yes. You could have had him shifted.'
'Really? How?'
'Man, he's an employee of Garths, isn't he? You know Andrew Garth. Something could have been arranged.'
'We prefer to do it our way.'
'So you've got yourselves a governess. A governess! For a girl of Laura's age!'
'What would you have us call her, then? A female tutor? That's what she is. All right, call her that, if it pleases you.'
'That's not what I mean, and you know it, James.' He paused. 'Besides, I should have thought you'd avoid governesses like the plague.'

James stiffened, shifting from his lounging position to rest his arms along the arms of his chair. 'Don't talk garbage!'

'Garbage, is it?' Now it was his father's turn to look amused. 'You didn't think so at the time.'

'Leave it!'

'I wonder what happened to her, hmm?' His father swung his chair in half turns. 'I wonder what would have happened if she hadn't gone away?'

James rose abruptly to this feet, walking impatiently towards the wide windows with their panoramic view of London's rooftops. 'That's an unnecessary speculation.'

'Nevertheless, I wonder what would have happened if Deborah had found out what was going on.'

'There was no question of Deborah finding out.'

'She might have done.'

'No. I took damn good care of that.'

Robert Booth shook his head. 'You puzzle me, James, you really do. In your position—' He broke off. 'Practically any one of the girls in the office, and those you meet socially . . . Man, don't you ever feel like—'

13

'What has this got to do with the Dryburn figures?'

'Nothing, nothing.' His father made a deprecating gesture. 'I'm sorry if you think I'm treading in deep water, but you're my son, James. I care about you. I care about the kind of life you're leading. It's not natural for a man of your age.'

'Oh, for God's sake!' James strode towards the door. 'All this, just because we're employing a governess for Laura.'

'Who is she? This governess? What's she like? Have you met her? Do you think she's a suitable companion for a girl as impressionable as Laura?'

'I know nothing about her except that she has exemplary references from her past employer. Laura needs tutoring in English, French and history. This woman can do it. What more need I know? I doubt if I'll even meet the woman above a couple of times.'

'Deborah interviewed her, I take it.'

'Yes.'

'Is she a young woman?'

'How the hell should I know? What does it matter? For the Lord's sake, Father, what do you expect me to do? Have a violent affair with every governess that comes my way?' He put his hand on the handle, and then hesitated, one clenched fist pressed against the panelling. 'Look, I admit that once ... But it was something I couldn't control. Thank heavens, she could. But that was the only time I ever ...' He breathed deeply. 'You ask what would have happened if she hadn't gone away. I don't know, I honestly don't. I've asked myself that question, and I guess I hope that I'd have had the sense to call it off after a while.'

Robert Booth nodded. 'But you took an appalling risk taking her away for the week-end, James. Why couldn't you have taken your pleasure in some hotel room during those long hot afternoons that summer?'

James looked back over his shoulder at his father, and

now there was a glimmer of reluctant amusement in his dark eyes. 'Do I have to answer that?' he asked.

Robert brought his hand down hard upon his desk, and then he gave a short laugh. 'No. No, I suppose not. But you were a fool, James.'

'I know.' James opened the door. 'Are you and Mother coming to dinner on Friday?'

'I don't think so. Your mother's got some Women's Guild affair on Saturday, and there'll be preparations to be made. I shall have to put off the pleasure of meeting your new governess.'

James looked impatient. 'Some pleasure,' he muttered bleakly.

But back in his own office, he could not quite dismiss the things his father had said. Employing a governess had necessarily brought memories of the past into his mind, and he supposed it was not unreasonable that his father should think of these things, too. After all, it had been, indirectly, because of his father that he had first encountered the only woman, apart from his mother, that he had ever really cared about. She had been doing some holiday cramming with the Forsters' two boys. The Forsters were friends of his father's, and as Arnold Forster preferred to work at home, James had been obliged to keep a business appointment with him there which his father had had to miss. It had seemed inevitable that he should meet the Forsters' governess. Not that anything had happened at that first meeting. She had known who he was, of course, the Booth name was not unknown, and she had known that he was a married man. She had been cool and polite, and nothing more would have happened if he had not gone out of his way to make it happen. He had never come up against anything he could not control before, never wanted any woman he could not have. For a time, he had toyed with the idea of asking Deborah for a divorce, but he knew he could not do that. Beside her extreme dependence upon him, there was Laura, then only ten years old. He had known that Deborah would never voluntarily agree to let him go, and if he should choose to walk out, he would never have free access to his daughter again. But still, he could not keep away from the girl, and their relationship had developed almost against her will. He had known she was attracted to him, and had used his not inconsiderable charm without scruple, arousing her emotions, teaching her with the expertise of his greater experience. Until that disastrous week-end when he persuaded her to go away with him . . .

He sighed suddenly and drew a tray of correspondence towards him. This was not getting his work done. Reminiscing about the past would help no one, even if there was still a certain amount of bitterness attached to remembrance. Nothing disastrous had happened, except that she had left him, and so far as he knew she was now teaching some class of comprehensive kids in one of the big co-educational schools. That had been her intention, although that summer he had known her, she had been only eighteen, waiting to start her first year at university. Eighteen! He pulled a wry face. Two years older than Laura was now, and he had been what? Thirty? Thirty-one? At least twelve years older than she was, and he was supporting Deborah in her assertion that John Mooney at twenty-five was too old for Laura. He shook his head. Was he a hypocrite? Was he the kind of man he had always despised, who denounced others for doing exactly what he would have liked to do? And he had been worse. At least Mooney was not married, or a father!

He pressed his finger hard down upon the inter-communication system. 'Mrs. Sully? Oh, yes. Will you come in, please?'

He released the switch and tried to concentrate on the letters in front of him, but a girl's face swam before his eyes – oval-shaped, huge green eyes, honey-blonde hair, straight, like strands of silk. Oh, God! he thought frustratedly, why had he allowed his father to talk about her?

She had been successfully banished to the realms of his subconscious. Just because Laura was going to have some middle-aged spinster teach her advanced studies it did not necessitate a re-examination of something best forgotten.

CHAPTER TWO

CAROLINE Douglas stood outside Reading station wondering what she would do if no one came to meet her as it had been arranged they should. She had no real address, just some nebulous mention of 'the house' as being a few miles from Reading, in country surroundings, not far from the river. Perhaps she should have asked for more details, but those she had been given had seemed explicit – at the time. She knew the name of her employer, the name of the girl she was to tutor, that the money was more than generous. What more had she needed to know?

But after all, she had not expected to get the job, and perhaps she would have asked more questions if she had not been so taken aback by her success. From the moment she had entered the ante-room adjoining the expensive suite of rooms in one of London's most luxurious hotels and seen the other short-listed applicants, she had felt convinced that her chances were negligible. The other women waiting to be interviewed had all appeared to possess far more aptitude and experience, and indeed, listening to their conversations, she gathered that most of them had been employed as governesses before, some of them with titled families. To Caroline, fresh from a post in a mission school in Sri Lanka, her qualifications seemed hardly worth consideration. In fact, she had wondered why they were even bothering to interview her, particularly as her name came last on the list.

But at last it had been her turn to enter the room where the interviews were being conducted, and a woman of indeterminate age, probably in her forties, Caroline had thought, and whose name was Mrs. Frobisher, asked her a lot of personal questions. How old was she? When had she first started teaching? Who were her first pupils? What university had she attended, and what posts had she had since then? The woman had seemed more interested in her background than in her actual teaching experience.

At the end of the interview, Caroline had rejoined the other women in the ante-room to await the appointment of the post, and had been absolutely astounded when after a few minutes Mrs. Frobisher had emerged and announced that she had got the job. There had been a few disgusted murmurs – after all, Caroline was barely twenty-four and looked younger, and it had been obvious that her qualifications could not possibly outweigh theirs. Caroline herself had been too stunned to offer any objections, and only later did she ponder the reasons why she should have been chosen. Still, the girl she was to tutor was sixteen and perhaps her parents preferred the idea of a younger companion. Whatever their reasons, she had got the job, and she had refused to worry any further about it.

Tim had been furious, of course, but she had expected that. After all, she had spent the last two years in Sri Lanka, and it was natural that he should object to her going away again, albeit the distance was vastly reduced. But after ten weeks of seeing him every day she had known she had to get away. She liked Tim, he was good fun, but she didn't love him and she never would. She didn't quite know how she knew this, but she did. He was the only man she had ever really liked, the only man she had ever had for a friend. But still she could not see herself spending the rest of her life with him. Generally speaking, she had no time for men. Men were predators, selfish, self-seeking individuals, who wanted everything without giving anything of themselves in return. In her teens, she had had a painful demonstration of this, and she had learned that particular lesson very well.

But now here she was, waiting outside Reading railway station, without any further information but that she would be met and driven to her destination by a man known as Groom, the Frobishers' chauffeur. And he was late. She consulted the square masculine watch encircling her slim wrist. Fifteen minutes late, to be exact.

'Miss Douglas?'

Engrossed in her thoughts, she had been unaware of anyone approaching her, and she looked up in surprise at the grey-uniformed figure confronting her. This had to be the chauffeur, Groom, she realized, a man of medium height, grey-haired, and presently looking rather apologetic.

'Yes?' Caroline's response was cool.

'Thank goodness for that!' Groom's grimace was comical, and Caroline felt a little more sympathetic towards him. 'I was half afraid you'd have got tired of waiting and wandered off somewhere. Mrs. Booth would have had my hide if I'd missed you.'

'Mrs. – Booth?' Caroline stiffened slightly, but then relaxed again. Mrs. Booth was probably the housekeeper. It wasn't such an uncommon name. It was just she was oversensitive to it.

'Yes, miss.' Groom looked down at the two suitcases standing side by side. 'Is this all your luggage, miss?'

Caroline took possession of the vanity case which held her personal belongings and nodded. 'Yes, that's all,' she answered, and Groom lifted a case in each hand.

'It's just round the corner, miss – the car, I mean. Will you come this way?'

Caroline's eyes widened expressively when she saw the long black Mercedes that awaited them. It was the kind of car she had hitherto only seen in the movies, and when she was installed in the back she felt like royalty. She had never known such space could exist inside a car, and a quiver of anticipation ran through her. The Frobishers must be extremely wealthy.

Groom climbed behind the wheel after stowing her cases in the boot, and slid down the screen that divided the compartments. 'Comfortable?' he asked, and she smiled.

'You've got to be joking!'

'Yes, it is spacious, isn't it. Beautiful mover, too. I've had a hundred and thirty out of it on the autobahn. Not over here, though. These roads weren't meant for it.'

Caroline acknowledged this, and Groom set the vehicle in motion, turning it expertly in the narrow side street. When they stopped at the first set of traffic lights, he went on:

'I should explain why I was late. It was Miss Laura. She's disappeared. We've been combing the grounds since two o'clock, but it's my guess she's gone into Fenbourne, little monkey.'

Caroline felt perturbed. 'Miss Laura? You mean the girl I'm here to teach?'

'Yes, miss. There's only one Miss Laura.'

'But does she make a habit of disappearing like this?'

'Oh, no, not usually. But – well, I suppose she's just lodging her protest, so to speak.'

'Lodging her protest?' Caroline shook her head. 'Look, I'm sorry if I seem dense, but why would she feel the need to protest?'

Groom glanced at her through the rear-view mirror. 'That's not for me to say, miss.'

'No. But having said so much, surely you can make an exception.'

Groom frowned. 'Oh, it's a storm in a teacup really. She doesn't take to the idea of having a governess. Not at her age.'

'I see.' Caroline digested this with resignation. She might have known it wasn't all going to be plain sailing. 'I gather I'm not the first, then.'

'Oh, you are, miss, oh yes.' Groom was very firm about this, negotiating the traffic with the ease of long experience. 'The young lady was at Boscombe last term. Went there when she was thirteen, she did.'

'Boscombe School?' Caroline had heard of the famous girls' school.

'That's right, miss.'

Caroline was tempted to ask the chauffeur outright why the girl was not going back there, but controlled herself. After all, there could be any number of reasons – she might even have been expelled. And if that was so, it did not augur well for peaceful relations.

'And why do you think she's gone to – Fenbourne? That was the place you mentioned, wasn't it?'

'Yes, miss. Well, I can't be sure, of course, but I'd say it was highly likely. There are telephone boxes in Fenbourne, and Miss Laura's a rare one for making calls, she is.'

Caroline's brow furrowed. 'You mean there's no phone at – at the house?'

Groom chuckled. 'Bless you, yes. Dozens of 'em, I suppose. But calls at the house are monitored by Mrs. French. She's Mr. Booth's housekeeper, and I—'

'Mr. Booth?' This time Caroline knew there could be no mistake in querying the name.

'Yes, miss. And Miss Laura, she likes to make her calls in private, you might—'

'Mr. *Booth*!' said Caroline again. 'Who – who is Mr. Booth?'

Groom glanced over his shoulder at her, and his expression was ludicrous. 'You kidding me?'

'No.' Caroline shook her head.

Groom frowned. 'And you are Miss Douglas? Miss Caroline Douglas? Bound for Maitlands?'

'Well, I didn't know exactly where I was bound for, but yes, I'm Caroline Douglas. Why?'

'Well, miss, if you don't mind my saying so, you should know who your employer is.'

'My – employer?'

'Yes, miss. Mr. Booth.'

'I was employed by somebody called Frobisher,' exclaimed Caroline faintly.

'Were you, miss?' Groom frowned. 'Oh, yes, that would be Mrs. Irene Frobisher. She's a great friend of Mrs. Booth, and Mrs. Booth being incapacitated like, she probably dealt with the interviews for her.'

Caroline felt slightly sick. 'Mrs. Booth is – incapacitated?' Her heart hammered heavily. 'You mean – she's confined to a wheelchair?'

'That was sharp of you, miss. Yes, as a matter of fact, she is. You've heard of her, I expect. I should have guessed, Mr. Booth being who he is and all.'

'Oh, yes.' Caroline licked dry lips. 'Yes, I've heard of her.'

Groom nodded, slowing the car as a group of schoolchildren were conducted across the road by an attendant. They were on the outskirts of Reading now. It could not be far to – what was it? – Maitlands? Yes, that was it. Maitlands. She had never known the name of his house, but then she hadn't really known too much about his personal affairs. He had seen to that.

'I—' She broke off as Groom's alert eyes encountered her through the reflection in the rear-view mirror.

'Yes, miss?'

'Oh, nothing.' Caroline drew a steadying breath, and tried to think coherently. God, what was she going to do? She had committed herself to working for the one man she had hoped never to see again in her life. But how had it happened? Had he known she would recognize the name and deliberately had this Mrs. Frobisher interview her to disguise it? Or did he imagine there might be more than one Caroline Douglas looking for a post as governess in London? What a coincidence if that were so! She had not long returned from Sri Lanka. The advertisement which she had read in *The Times* could not have appeared more aptly. He must have known. He must have contrived this. That was why she had been appointed to the post instead of any one of the other, more suitable, applicants. But what was his game? How dared he introduce into his own home the girl he had once tried to make his mistress? Had he no shame? Didn't he care that she might go to his wife and tell her of their previous association? What a despicable thing to do!

She shifted uneasily in her seat. What could she do about it? She had been paid the month's probationary salary in advance, and some of that money had already been spent. She had earned only a small salary in Sri Lanka, and coming back to England's cooler climate she had needed new clothes. Besides, there had been her temporary lodging to pay for, and even when she gave that up a week before taking this post, and moved in with Tim, there had still been food to pay for. Without any of the luxuries which nowadays were treated as necessities. She would have liked to have asked Groom to turn and drive her back to the station, but how could she?

Outside they were passing fields, green with ripening corn, hedges bright with meadowsweet and the scarlet splashes of poppies. It was a warm May afternoon and she should have been enjoying the prospect of working for the next few months in surroundings, which, if they matched this car, promised to be very comfortable indeed. But all she could think was that she was confined, trapped, enmeshed – by fate's, or a more tangible, hand – in the coils of a dilemma from which for the moment there seemed no escape. What a beastly situation, and how twisted the mind which had devised it?

Groom was watching her through his mirror. Caroline became aware of his curious scrutiny with a start, and guessed he was wondering what was causing such a shift of emotions across her suddenly pale features, pale beneath the tan she had acquired with so little effort in the hills above Kandy. With a determined effort she endeavoured to school her expression, concentrating instead on the small village she could see ahead of them.

'Er – where is this?' she inquired, with remarkable composure.

'This is Fenbourne,' announced Groom, looking about him searchingly, no doubt hoping to observe the missing teenager. 'Nice little place. You can get a decent meal at the Coach and Horses if you feel like a break of an evening.'

'Thank you.' Caroline thought dryly that she might well need several breaks. Then, refusing to allow the deepening depression of her thoughts, she went on: 'Is it far from – from Maitlands?'

'Matter of two or three miles, no more. Miss Laura cycles down here sometimes. Been on at her father to get one of those Hondas, she has. You know, those motorbikes all the youngsters seem to ride these days, but he wouldn't allow it. Not surprised really. She's a wild little thing, Miss Laura. Come to grief, she would, like as not.'

Caroline's fingers tortured the strap of her bag. 'Is – er – is Mr. Booth a – a strict parent?'

Groom chuckled. 'Sometimes, miss, sometimes. But he thinks the world of Miss Laura. You've no need to worry there, miss. He's a good employer, fair but firm, as they say. You'll have no trouble with him, if that's what you're thinking about.'

Wouldn't she? Caroline wished she could feel so confident. Of course, Groom thought she was concerned about her working conditions. If only that was all she had to think about!

The car turned a bend in the road and ahead of them Caroline could see a high brick wall that followed the line of the road for some distance before breaking into tall wrought iron gates that were closed against them.

'Here we are, miss. Maitlands,' announced the chauffeur, sounding his horn as they approached. There was a lodge by the gates, and a man came out to check on the identity of the visitors. Recognizing Groom, he raised a hand in greeting before going back inside the lodge and releasing some mechanism which set the gates in motion. 'Electrically controlled,' Groom added unnecessarily. 'Can't be too careful these days.'

'No.' As the car passed through the gates and began the gradual ascent to the house, Caroline felt another shiver of apprehension. A prison indeed, she thought uneasily.

And then her apprehensions were temporarily dispersed as she caught her first glimpse of the house. It was a stone structure, its grey walls overhung with ivy, while clematis climbed up columns that supported a wide terrace. The windows were tall and arched, the roof sported what appeared to be an immense amount of chimney stacks, and two solid doors stood wide to the porch beyond. Shallow steps led up to the terrace, and at this hour of the afternoon sunlight cast lengthening shadows from the urns spilling over with fuchsias and geraniums that flanked the columns. It lived up to all her expectations of what a house should be, and she would not have been human if she had not felt a sense of pleasure in its appearance. And then, as a figure in a wheelchair came out through the open double doors, she was transported back to reality with a jerk.

Groom brought the car to a halt at the foot of the terrace steps with a swish of wheels on gravel. Then he got out, raised his cap to the woman in the wheelchair, and opened the rear door for Caroline to alight. Caroline got out more slowly. Her nerves felt tight and strung up, and she had no idea what to expect from this first interview. She glanced down automatically to assure herself that her skirt was not creased, and was glad she had not succumbed to the temptation to wear pants for travelling. Her fine wool suit was plain but well styled, and suitable apparel for a governess, she had thought. Equally, her hair was drawn back, madonna-like, from her face, and apart from two strands which curled by her ears was coiled at the nape of her neck.

The wheelchair rolled to within a foot of the shallow

steps and Caroline felt an instinctive desire to draw it back which she managed to control as the other woman called: 'Come up, Miss Douglas. As you can see, it's rather difficult for me to come down.'

Glancing back at Groom who was busying himself taking her cases out of the boot, Caroline decided she had no choice but to obey, and on slightly jelly-like legs she climbed to the terrace. Mrs. Booth held out her hand. 'How do you do, Miss Douglas? It's so nice to meet you at last.'

'How – how do you do?' Caroline shook hands politely, despising herself for not wanting to touch the woman who was his wife. But she was beautiful, there was no denying that. And she wondered anew how he could do such a thing – to his wife.

'Did you have a good journey?' Mrs. Booth was speaking again. 'I'm sorry Groom wasn't on time to meet you, but no doubt he's explained we had a little fracas here.'

'He – he did say something.'

'I knew he would.' Groom came up the steps just then with Caroline's cases, and Mrs. Booth switched her attention to him for a moment. 'Just take them into the hall, Groom. Mrs. French will deal with them. Thank you.'

Groom acknowledged his instructions and then the woman returned her attention to Caroline. 'Come along inside, won't you? You must be dying for a cup of tea or something long and cool to drink, aren't you? Such lovely weather. I hope it lasts.'

The wheelchair glided ahead of Caroline, over the specially arched threshold and into a wide cool hall, panelled in oak. There was a peach-coloured carpet on the floor, sweeping up the wide staircase, and several small prints on the walls which Caroline would have liked to have examined further. But Mrs. Booth was leading the way into a large living-room, and Caroline's attention was soon distracted by a row of exquisite miniatures lining the marble mantelshelf above a screened fireplace.

The other woman, noticing her interest, asked: 'Are you a collector of antiques, Miss Douglas?'

Caroline gave a swift shake of her head. 'I know very little about them, I'm afraid. But they're so beautiful.' She indicated the tiny portraits. 'Who are they?'

'I don't know their names, but they were the children of the painter, Lascal. He worked in the late eighteenth and early nineteenth centuries, and was fortunate enough to be known and respected in his own lifetime. So many of our most famous painters today were never recognized in their own time.'

'No.' Caroline dragged her attention away from the miniatures. 'This is a beautiful room.'

And it was. A creamy pink carpet was a perfect foil for dark wood furniture, much of it antique or reproduction, Caroline thought, and the cream and gold striped walls were obviously silk-hung. There was an ebony cabinet filled with jade, and the chess pieces occupying a giant board were definitely ivory. It was the kind of room Caroline had hitherto only seen on film or in some stately home, and it was not really a place in which one could relax.

'I'm so glad you like it,' Mrs. Booth was saying now, turning her chair as someone cleared their throat in the doorway. 'Ah, Mrs. French. Miss Douglas, I'd like you to meet our housekeeper. Mrs. French, will you see that Miss Douglas's suitcases are taken up to her room, and we'd like some tea.' She glanced back at Caroline. 'Or would you prefer something stronger?'

'Tea would be fine,' Caroline assured her quickly, and the housekeeper withdrew again. She seemed a taciturn woman, tall and thin and dark, without any of the buxom features one associated with country housekeepers, and she had not addressed a word of welcome to the new governess. Caroline couldn't help wondering what her relationship with the other staff would be like. If she stayed ...

'Won't you sit down?' Mrs. Booth indicated a Regency striped chair. 'You make me feel at quite a disadvantage, standing there. You're quite tall, aren't you, Miss Douglas?'

Caroline instantly subsided into the chair indicated. 'I'm five feet eight,' she supplied automatically. 'Er – Mrs. Booth...'

'Yes?' The woman's dark brows arched interrogatively, and Caroline made a helpless gesture. What could she say?

'I – did – did you find your daughter?' she asked lamely.

'Laura? Oh, yes, eventually. She'd been – cycling. I've told her that in future she must tell us where she's going.'

'I see.' Caroline shifted in her seat. 'About the – the interview...'

'Yes?'

'I – I understood that Mrs. Frobisher—'

'You thought Irene was to be your employer? Oh, no, how could you get that idea? Didn't she explain?'

'I'm afraid not.'

'Oh, that's too bad, too bad.' The woman seemed genuinely concerned. Then: 'Does it make a difference? I can assure you, our background is just as creditable as the Frobishers'.'

'I'm sure it is, but—'

'Miss Douglas.' The woman opposite her sighed deeply. 'Miss Douglas, you see what I am, don't you? A helpless invalid, forced to spend the rest of my days in this contraption. An ugly cripple. No, wait—' this as Caroline would have protested, 'you don't know what it's like, Miss Douglas. Being wholly dependent upon other people, self-conscious of one's afflictions, reluctant to lay oneself open to well-meaning compassion and pity!' She shook her head. 'I avoid meeting strangers. I can't bear being patronised. Oh, you may think I'm foolish and selfish, perhaps, but that's the way I'm made.' She paused. 'Consequently, when the interviews for this post came up,

I couldn't do it. I couldn't take them. Fortunately Mrs. Frobisher, who is a dear friend of mine, offered to take them for me. Please don't feel annoyed because there was some innocent mix-up over names. I assure you, Laura is desperately in need of academic supervision, and I'm looking forward to having someone young to talk to.'

Caroline made a helpless gesture. 'I – I just wonder if I have the qualifications necessary—'

'I'm perfectly happy with your qualifications, Miss Douglas, and so, too, is my husband.' She paused again, and Caroline looked down at her hands folded in her lap as faint colour spread up her cheeks. 'You're exactly what Laura needs,' Mrs. Booth went on reassuringly. 'Someone young and adaptable, someone who will be her friend as well as her governess.'

Caroline could not think of anything to say in answer to this and it was perhaps fortunate that Mrs. French chose that moment to return wheeling a tray on which reposed a delicate china tea service, and several dishes containing wafer-thin sandwiches, cakes and small pastries.

'Ah, tea.' Mrs. Booth indicated that the housekeeper should wheel the trolley near her chair. 'Thank you, Mrs. French. Is Miss Douglas's room ready?'

'Yes, madam.' Mrs. French straightened and stood with her hands linked together over her apron. 'Shall I send Jenny through later on to take Miss Douglas upstairs?'

'Please.'

The housekeeper was dismissed and Caroline's employer contemplated the trolley. 'This looks very nice. Do help yourself, Miss Douglas. Let me see – these sandwiches are salmon and cucumber, and those are pâté. Which would you prefer?'

In truth, Caroline thought she would have great difficulty in swallowing anything, but as the sandwiches seemed the least unacceptable, she took a paté wafer and smiled her thanks. Mrs. Booth poured the tea, and as she did so Caroline studied her more closely. There was no trace of nervousness in the way she handled the teapot, and not a drop of tea landed anywhere other than in the cup. Which was surprising considering her assertion that she was chary of meeting strangers. But perhaps meeting an employee on her home ground was different from interviewing a dozen women in the alien environment of an hotel. Caroline could honestly see no reason why she should feel uneasy with strangers. Without the knowledge that her chair was a wheelchair, one could be forgiven for assuming that she was a normal, attractive woman in her late thirties. Slim, dark hair styled by an expert hand, and with the kind of skin that careful use of cosmetics had kept unlined, she inspired admiration rather than pity. In her youth, in the days before the tragic accident which had crippled her spine, she would have attracted a great number of ardent admirers. Including James Booth, Caroline reminded herself bitterly. He had married her. And then, when he had grown bored with playing nursemaid to an invalid wife, he had looked elsewhere for his pleasures.

'I understand you've just returned from India, Miss Douglas,' Mrs. Booth was saying now. 'Does that account for that marvellous tan? I'm sure you couldn't acquire one like it in England.'

Caroline forced herself to behave naturally. 'I – it was Ceylon, actually. Sri Lanka. Yes, I've just been back a couple of months.'

'And did you like it over there?'

'It was very hot most of the time. Very humid. But it was an experience.'

'Yes.' The older woman sipped reflectively at her tea. 'Do you enjoy – experiences, Miss Douglas?'

Caroline frowned. 'I don't quite—'

'I'm sorry.' Mrs. Booth smiled apologetically. 'I phrased that badly. What I should have said was, do you like adventures, that kind of adventure.'

'Oh, I see.' Caroline shrugged. 'I thought it would be interesting working in a foreign country.'

'And it was?'

'Yes. But it's nice to be home again.'

'You have a home?' Mrs. Booth frowned. 'I thought – Mrs. Frobisher led me to understand—'

'Oh, no, I see what you mean. England is my home. That's what I meant. But you're right, I have no real home here. My parents died when I was ten, and I spent the next seven or eight years of my life in foster homes. Then – then I went to university.'

'To Oxford – I believe.'

'Well, yes.'

'Very clever!'

Caroline flushed. 'Not really. It's just that I enjoy studying.'

'And what hobbies do you have, Miss Douglas? What – turns you on, as they say?'

Caroline hesitated. 'Not a lot. I enjoy books, and music. And I've swum a lot in Sri Lanka. I like swimming.'

'Well, we have a pool here.' Mrs. Booth gestured towards the garden, visible beyond the long windows. 'My husband uses it often.' She paused, and Caroline made an effort to show enthusiasm for the cup of tea in her hand. 'There's also an indoor pool, in the basement. I use it as part of my therapy, but if ever you would care to join me—'

'Thank you.' Caroline could think of nothing else to say.

'What about – boy-friends?'

'I – no.' Caroline was uneasy again. 'No one serious, that is.' How Tim would hate to hear her say that!

'Good, good.' Mrs. Booth smiled again, and Caroline felt warmed by her friendliness. 'I think we should get along together very well, Miss Douglas. You're exactly what Laura needs, what we all need.' She indicated the teapot. 'Now, may I offer you some more tea?'

Caroline refused, and for a few moments there was silence. Then Caroline felt compelled to ask: 'When will I meet – Laura, Mrs. Booth?'

The older woman's laugh was light and musical. 'Of course. Naturally you're eager to meet your pupil, Miss Douglas. I've enjoyed our conversation so much, I almost forgot the reasons for you being here.'

Caroline could hardly believe this, but she let it go. Then, deciding it would be more tactful not to mention Groom's gossiping in the car, she said: 'Has your daughter had other governesses, Mrs. Booth?'

'Actually, no.' The woman hesitated. 'Didn't Mrs. Frobisher explain? Laura has been at boarding school, but just before Easter she developed pneumonia. She'd foolishly been caught out without a coat in a storm, and my husband and I decided it might be less strenuous for her to be taught at home for a while.'

'I see. But she's recovered now.'

'Oh, yes, she's quite fit. But you know how it is when parents have only one child. They positively dote on her, and I'm afraid Laura can twist us both round her little finger.'

That didn't quite tie up with what Groom had said, but Caroline was astute enough to realize that parents didn't always see things the way other people did. What disturbed her more was the knowledge that James had lied to her about Laura, too. He had always maintained that his wife had no time for the child, that Laura would suffer if he was ever foolish enough to ask for a divorce, that he would seldom be allowed to see the child again. She remembered what he had said very well. It had once seemed the only redeeming feature in his otherwise selfish behaviour.

'Of course,' the older woman was going on, 'I'm not saying that Laura entirely approves of our arrangements on her behalf. She's an – independent little thing, and thinks we're making far too much fuss over her illness. But there you are. Parents are like that, aren't they?' Then she broke off. 'Oh, I'm sorry, Miss Douglas. You wouldn't know, would you? That was – careless of me.'

Later the maid, Jenny, appeared to take Caroline up to her room, and it was with some relief that Caroline followed her up the stairs to the first floor. She still had no idea whose suggestion it had been that Laura should have a governess, and her position, if anything, had deteriorated. But what could she do about it? Without revealing her real reasons for wanting to leave Maitlands minutes after her arrival?

Her room was at the end of a corridor branching to the left at the head of the staircase. To the right, a beautifully carved balustrade formed a landing which looked down on the hall below before itself extending into another wing of the house. Doors opened off this landing, and between were further examples of antique art. As she came up the stairs, Caroline had noticed an enormous Chinese vase standing on the landing above, filled with pampas-grass, whose silvery plume-like flowers caught the last rays of the sun, and she had realized how little she knew or understood of people who lived in such exotic surroundings.

The room which had been allotted to her was huge. A high sculpted ceiling looked down on a square, four-poster bed whose canopy matched the creamy silk curtains at the windows, and the cream and gold coverings on the bed itself. There was a gilt-edged escritoire, where she could prepare the work for the following day, a comfortable armchair facing a colour television, and a small, circular table and ladder-backed chair had been set in the window embrasure, no doubt where she was expected to take most of her meals. The long windows which presently stood wide to the rapidly cooling air overlooked the gardens at the back of the house. Away to the right she could see a vegetable garden with peas and beans climbing up their canes, while below her the terrace opened on to lawns and a rose garden, and beyond there was a wrought iron trellis and the glint of green water, which probably signified the presence of the pool. The pool that James used often ...

She turned back to face the room again, and pushing such disturbing thoughts aside, explored further. The bathroom which adjoined the bedroom-cum-living room was equally elegant. Cream and gold tiles on the floor, honey-coloured bath and basin incorporating a shower, and mirror-lined walls which struck her as being slightly indecent. A cabinet revealed a comprehensive array of bath salts, lotions and talc; everything in fact to enhance the delights of relaxing in warm scented water, and with a feeling of desperation, Caroline turned on the taps. Perhaps a bath would cool her brain and allow her to analyse the alternatives she was faced with.

CHAPTER THREE

THE bath did little to restore Caroline's failing confidence, and she rummaged through the cases which Mrs. French had had brought to her room with a reckless disregard for their contents. Mrs. Booth had asked that she should join herself and her husband, and incidentally Laura, in the library at seven o'clock. Caroline didn't altogether know what this summons meant – whether in fact it was simply a case of being introduced to the master of the household and her pupil, or whether she was expected to join them for dinner. Either way, she decided, a pants suit offered the safest solution, and she was brushing her hair at the dressing-table mirror, prior to getting dressed, when there was a knock at her door.

Immediately, her nerves tightened to screaming pitch, and she was convinced that if James himself should be beyond that door, she would walk out of this house right there and then, without caring that she might be arrested for taking money under false pretences. Maybe she was being over-dramatic, six years was a long time, after all, but she remembered everything that had happened with a clarity that denied the passage of time.

'Yes?'

Her voice was reassuringly brusque, and weakness enveloped her as a young, female voice called: 'Can I come in?'

Caroline's brow furrowed, and dropping the hairbrush, she reached for the silk robe she had worn when she came out of the bath. 'I – yes. Come in.'

The girl who entered had to be James's daughter. She was so like him that Caroline felt an actual shock of recognition. Slim, straight dark hair, with the same deep-set brown eyes and olive complexion. Her mother was dark, too, of course, but it was a much gentler strain. Laura was all Booth. She came into the room, glancing about her defensively, as though half afraid that Caroline was not alone, and then, after closing the door, she said: 'Hello. I'm Laura.'

Caroline's fingers curled into her palms in the pockets of her gown as she confronted the jean-clad figure. 'Yes, I thought perhaps you might be.'

Laura gave a brief smile. 'And you're Miss Douglas, of course. I saw you arrive.'

'You saw me?'

'From my bedroom window,' Laura explained quickly. 'It overlooks the drive. I've been confined there since I got back from Fenbourne earlier on.'

Caroline could feel her eyes widening. 'Really?'

'Yes, really. Didn't Mummy tell you? Groom was apparently late in going to meet you. Because of me.'

'She might have said something about it.' Caroline had no intention of taking sides in this affair.

'I expect she did. She'd have to give you some reason for your not meeting me, wouldn't she?'

'Not necessarily,' replied Caroline mildly. 'I understood I was to meet you later this evening.'

'Oh!' The wind was temporarily dashed from her sails. But not for long. 'Well, anyway, I wanted to speak to you first. I wanted you to know that I don't want, or need, a governess! If I can't complete my schooling in the way all my friends are completing theirs, then I don't intend to learn anything more, and you'll be wasting your time thinking I will!'

'Indeed?' Caroline felt a reluctant sense of admiration for her forthrightness. Some might call it insolence, but Laura was not being insolent. She was merely stating the facts, as she saw them. 'Don't you think your parents deserve more consideration than this?'

'My parents!' Laura hunched her shoulders 'Look, I don't know what my mother's told you, but I can guess. I don't suppose she happened to mention Johnny, did she?'

'Johnny?' Caroline's instinctive echoing of the name was enough.

'No, I thought not. I expect she gave you that story about me developing pneumonia, and having to be sent home from school.'

'And weren't you?' Caroline couldn't suppress the question.

'What? Oh, yes. Yes.' Laura scuffed her canvas-clad toe against the carpet. 'Yes, I did have the illness. But I'm perfectly well now!'

'I can see that,' commented Caroline dryly. 'Even so—'

'Even so, nothing. Oh, Miss Douglas, if I tell you about Johnny, will you think seriously about resigning from this post?'

'Resigning?' Caroline was shocked. Until this moment, that had been the thing she most desired to do. But put baldly like that – it was shocking somehow. Besides, until she could think of some way of returning the money she had spent . . . 'Laura, I don't think this is entirely ethical,' she said at last. 'I mean, your parents have employed me, and – well, I don't think they would approve of your talking to me like this.'

'But you have to understand, you have to know why you've been brought here!'

'I know why.' But did she?

'No, you don't.' Laura was adamant. 'Oh, all right, I'll tell you anyway. They're keeping me away from school because I've fallen in love with a young man who's working on the stretch of motorway they're building near the school!'

'Laura, please!' Caroline was aghast. 'I don't want to know.'

'Why not? You're bound to find out sooner or later if you stay here, because I won't give him up. So there!'

Caroline stared at the girl facing her so rebelliously and sighed. So that was what it was all about, was it? It made so much more sense than the hangover from some past illness somehow. A young man working on a motorway would not sound at all suitable as a friend for the youngest member of the Booth family. She could almost feel a sneaking sympathy for him, even while she appreciated that Laura was too young yet to be in love with anyone.

'And – er – what does he do, this young man?' she queried, curious in spite of herself.

Laura's voice became warm and enthusiastic. 'He's an engineer. His name's John Mooney, and he comes from Dublin.'

'Dublin?' echoed Caroline dryly. Then: 'But if he's an engineer, surely he must be quite a bit older than you are.'

Laura's expression grew mutinous again, and her eyes flashed angrily. 'So what? What's age got to do with it? It's the way you feel that matters.'

Caroline sighed. 'I assume from that that you've already had this argument from your parents.'

'They don't understand. They're too old—'

'Isn't that a bit too easy to say? They may understand better than you do.'

'Oh, you would say that, wouldn't you?' Laura's voice rose sharply in her disappointment. 'You're on their side, too. I should have known better than to think that anyone my mother employed would—'

'Laura, what the hell do you think you're doing?' The door to Caroline's bedroom was suddenly thrust open, and a dark attractive man stood glaring at the younger girl from the opening. 'I can hear your voice down the other end of the corridor,' he told her furiously. 'How dare you come in here disturbing—' His eyes shifted to the other occupant of the room, and then narrowed in arrant disbelief. '*Caroline!*' he muttered, and then controlled himself with what she sensed was an immense effort of will.

Realizing that Laura had now turned to look at her new governess with speculative curiosity, Caroline knew that something was expected of her. 'He – hello, Mr.

Booth,' she managed, with a coolness she had not known she possessed. 'How nice to see you again.'

'You two know each other?'

Laura's surprised statement gave them both a moment to assess the situation, and had Caroline not felt such an increasing sense of anger and resentment at the sight of his tall, lean figure, she might have admired James's instantaneous recovery. His fleeting lapse might never have been as he switched his attention back to his daughter and said:

'Miss Douglas and I met years ago, when she was doing some part-time tutoring. But that's beside the point, Laura. I demand an explanation for your behaviour.'

Laura pursed her lips. 'I'm sorry if you overheard me. I was just putting – Miss Douglas in the picture.'

James looked down at his daughter sternly, and Caroline, watching them, felt a stirring remembrance of pain inside her. This was *his* house; *his* wife, *his* child. And he had been prepared to put them all in jeopardy for the sake of a few hours spent in *her* bed. Of course, in those days, she had wanted it, too. At least for a time. Until common sense and decency had opened her eyes.

'Go to your room, Laura,' he was saying now, 'and change into something suitable, and then join your mother and Miss Douglas and me downstairs in the library, do you understand?'

'I'm not hungry,' muttered Laura sulkily.

'Nevertheless, you will do as I ask. Or do you want Miss Douglas to think you younger than she already believes?'

'Oh! Oh, all right.'

Laura flounced out of the room, and James accompanied her as far as the corridor immediately outside. Then he halted and looked back at Caroline. 'I'm sorry,' he said formally. 'Laura is quite a handful, as you can see.'

'Yes.' Caroline could think of nothing else to reply.

James stared at her a moment longer, and then he moved his shoulders within the expensive dark suit he was wearing in a gesture almost of dismissal. 'Excuse me. My wife is waiting for me.'

He strode away and Caroline rushed across the room to slam the door, leaning against it trembling. She was shocked and confused, and for several minutes she just lay there, fighting for composure. Then at last she straightened and went across to the dressing table, picking up her hairbrush again. Her face looked exactly the same, she thought dazedly, tugging the brush through the heavy curtain of hair, except that she was rather paler now than she had been when first she came out of the bath. But surely something should show, some physical mark of the pain which had torn through her at the sight of him. Hatred showed in the eyes, they said, but her eyes looked only bewildered. And yet she hated him more now than she had ever done before.

It was after seven by the time Caroline had completed her toilet and gone downstairs. Her hands had been trembling so badly she had smudged her eye-shadow on her cheeks, and she had tried to wind up one lipstick without taking off the cap. Then she had spilt her favourite perfume over the carpet, and now her room smelled like a scent distillery. Still, at last she was ready, slim and unconsciously appealing in black velvet trousers and a matching waistcoat, a long-sleeved white blouse with a froth of lace in front adding a touch of femininity to an otherwise masculine outfit. Her hair, as usual, was coiled at her nape, and she looked cool and, she hoped, more sophisticated than she felt.

Mrs. French was in the hall when she came downstairs, and directed her to the library. A door, faced with leather, confronted her, and her first tentative tap was absorbed by the cloth. Hearing the murmur of voices beyond, she tapped again, more loudly this time, and presently the door was opened for her, and she saw James Booth for the second time that day. He acknowledged her presence with a faint nod of his head, and she shifted her attention to the woman in the wheelchair, seated to the right of a huge wood-framed fireplace. Mrs. Booth saw her, and beckoned her forward.

'Come in, Miss Douglas,' she exclaimed encouragingly. 'We were just talking about you. I'm sorry you've had this trouble with Laura already.'

'It was no trouble.' Caroline reluctantly entered the book-lined room, fixing her attention on an enormous globe which had been half opened to reveal an impressive array of drinks inside. 'I'm sorry if I've kept you waiting.'

'Not at all.' This evening the older woman was elegant in a long red gown studded with sequins at the neckline and hem. 'Sit down, won't you, and have a drink? My husband has been telling me he has already met you.'

Caroline could feel the revealing colour sliding up her cheeks, but there was nothing she could do to stop it. 'Has he?' she murmured, rather inanely.

'Yes.' The woman who was James's wife looked teasingly up at her husband as he stood beside the opened globe, swallowing the last dregs of liquid from his glass. 'Haven't you, darling?'

Caroline's nails dug into her palms. What did she mean? What had James been telling her? That he had met her just now in that scene over Laura? Or – before?

He lowered his glass and his eyes met Caroline's over its rim, inscrutable, enigmatic eyes, that gave nothing away. 'I explained that you were the young lady employed by the Forsters some years ago to tutor Geoffrey and Vincent,' he stated coolly.

'Yes.' His wife took up the strain. 'What a coincidence! The Forsters are great friends of my father-in-law, my husband's father, that is. I'm sure he'll be surprised when he finds that you're Laura's governess, won't he, James?'

'Very surprised,' agreed James slowly. 'Now, Miss

Douglas, can I offer you a drink?'

Caroline hesitated and then she nodded. 'Th – thank you. I'll have a Martini, if I may.'

'Have something stronger,' suggested Mrs. Booth smoothly. 'That is ...' She paused. 'I just meant, after that run-in with Laura, you might feel in need of something more stimulating.'

'No. No, a Martini will be fine,' Caroline assured her quickly, and James added ice to her glass before pouring the colourless liquid. As he attended to his task, Caroline watched him with a rising feeling of animosity. His manner had convinced her that he was entirely without conscience for what he had done, and indignation brought a rush of courage which was as determined as it was fleeting. With deliberate affection, she said: 'I'm surprised you remember me at all, Mr. Booth. Our acquaintance was of such – short duration.'

As soon as the words were uttered, she wondered how she had had the nerve to say them, but at least she had the satisfaction of seeing that they had disconcerted him, too. His wife had listened to what Caroline had had to say with interest, and now she intervened.

'That's quite a point, Miss Douglas,' she murmured. 'James darling, are you trying to make me jealous?'

It was all said in a teasing bantering tone, but James took his own method of defence. 'I hate to disillusion you both, Deborah, but I met Irene Frobisher in town this afternoon. She mentioned Miss Douglas's name, and it was that, and not her undoubtedly charming face, which rang a bell.'

His wife's lips had tightened somewhat by the time he had finished, and Caroline felt suitably set down. But that didn't stop her from feeling angry and resentful, and when she took the glass he offered from his outstretched fingers, she allowed her feelings to show in the stormy depths of her eyes. If James noticed, he gave no sign, and moved to stand beside the empty fireplace, one foot raised to rest on the copper fender.

There was silence for a few minutes, and then Deborah Booth changed the subject, much to Caroline's relief. 'Tell me, Miss Douglas, exactly what was Laura saying to you?'

Caroline sighed. She was as loath to discuss Laura's confidence with her mother as she had been to discuss Laura's parents with the girl. 'I imagine you can guess,' she temporized slowly. 'It was an argument she had had before, I'm sure.'

'Mmm.' The older woman drew her lower lip between her teeth. 'I suppose she told you about this man, Mooney.'

'Yes.'

'A most unfortunate affair.' Deborah Booth's nostrils flared. 'How dare this man, this Irish navvy, consider himself Laura's equal!'

'I don't think that's quite the point, Deborah,' put in James quietly. 'Mooney's background is the least of our worries.' He paused. 'Surely, the whole point is that Laura is too young to get involved with anybody, much less a man almost ten years her senior!'

Caroline found his eyes upon her then, and she thought they were defying her to state that the difference in *their* ages had not mattered to *him*. But she couldn't do it. She argued with herself that to blurt something out like that would hurt the innocent far more than the guilty; but if she was honest she had to admit that she did not feel herself qualified to act as judge and jury on a fellow human being, however much she despised him.

'Nevertheless,' Deborah was saying now, 'the situation is impossible. Not content with causing the child to develop pneumonia, he pursues her here, to Fenbourne, constantly causing friction in the household!'

'Deborah developing pneumonia was incidental,' James began, but his wife interrupted him.

'I would hardly call pneumonia incidental, James!'

'You know what I mean. Two people caught out in a storm – she might well have been with a girl friend. The fact that she wasn't, that she was with this man Mooney, hardly makes him responsible.'

'All right. Be that as it may, the fact remains that she did get pneumonia and for a time she was very seriously ill.'

'I'll grant you that.'

'Thank you.' Deborah turned her attention back to Caroline. 'And now, today, she's been meeting this man in Fenbourne.'

'Oh!' Caroline's lips formed the letter.

'This man's an absolute pest. Doesn't he have a job of work to do?'

James went to pour himself another Scotch. 'He's an engineer, Deborah. I checked with the construction company he works for.'

'But if he's working on the motorway near Boscombe, what is he doing seventy miles away in Fenbourne?'

'I imagine he has days off,' remarked James dryly. 'Would you like another drink, Miss Douglas?'

As Caroline had scarcely touched the drink in her hand, she shook her head, but Deborah was obviously not interested in such mundane things.

'Whatever he is, Laura's got to learn that for the time being we will not allow her to do as she likes!' she stated sharply. 'Men of his age are only interested in girls of Laura's age for one thing and one thing only. And once they've got ...' She paused and looked directly at Caroline. 'Isn't that so, Miss Douglas? I'm sure you, with your greater experience, know exactly what I mean.'

Caroline's mouth felt so dry she felt incapable of making any sensible response. 'I – I—'

'Haven't you ever come up against this sort of thing, Miss Douglas?' Deborah persisted, and Caroline felt weak with relief when the library door suddenly opened and Laura herself appeared.

She had made some small concession to the occasion.

She had changed the jeans for smart pants, but the tee-shirt she was wearing with them with its flagrant message to *Turn me on, Baby* was hardly conducive to promoting good relations with her parents. Still, her arrival did divert Deborah's attention from Caroline, and Caroline ran each moist palm in turn surreptitiously over the seat of her pants. During Deborah's catechism, James had been standing silently beside the globe, but at his daughter's entrance he took up his position again before the hearth.

'Well?' challenged Laura, looking round at all of them. 'Here I am! Don't stop talking about me just because I'm here!'

'Your immaturity is only exceeded by your conceit,' her father told her quietly, and Caroline saw the way his words burst the girl's bubble of self-confidence.

'Weren't you talking about me, then?' she exclaimed, reverting to the rebellious tone she had used in Caroline's bedroom.

'We were discussing the probable intentions of a mature man with a schoolgirl,' returned Deborah quellingly. 'Miss Douglas was about to tell us her experience.'

'I doubt whether Miss Douglas's experiences could have any bearing in this case,' James remarked brusquely. 'Miss Douglas's behaviour is not under question here, Deborah, and I suggest we confine ourselves to the matter in hand.'

Caroline was reluctantly grateful for this respite, although she had the feeling that Deborah Booth would not be content to leave it there. But in spite of her relief, her antagonism towards the man who thought he could so easily dismiss any awkwardness in this situation increased.

Laura shifted restlessly. 'That's all you can think about, isn't it?' she burst out angrily. 'Sex and money. Money and sex!'

Deborah's hands clenched on the arms of her chair. 'Using silly phrases like that in an effort to shock people into listening to you is not going to solve anything, Laura,' she said coldly.

'They're not silly phrases. They're true. That's all you really worry about. Not me, and my happiness. Just whether he's laid me and how much he's going to squeeze out of you because of it!'

'Laura!'

Deborah turned horrified eyes on her husband, and even Caroline found her eyes drawn to Laura's father. He shook his head, almost imperceptibly, and then he said steadily:

'And has he? Lain with you, I mean?'

Laura's cheeks burned scarlet. But she was still defiant. 'Oh, yes. That sounds much more acceptable, doesn't it? Lain *with* me! Yes, he's lain *with* me. We were lying together this afternoon beside the river—'

James's fingers stung across Laura's cheek, and she raised her hand to cover the tell-tale marks, her mouth opening in silent protest. 'Go to your room!' James's voice was ice-cold. 'I'll speak to you later.'

Laura whirled and rushed out of the library, and Caroline heard the sounds of sobbing as she took the stairs two by two. There was another silence, pregnant with tension, and then James went to pour himself another Scotch, saying as he raised the glass to his lips: 'Be it ever so humble, there's no place like home!'

'That was unforgivable, James.'

Deborah was fingering the pearls about her throat with a restlessness which belied the calmness of her words, and for a moment Caroline thought she meant his slapping Laura's face. But a minute later she realized her mistake as Deborah went on:

'That a daughter of mine should stand there and actually admit to—' She broke off abruptly. 'I've always thought that that school allowed too much freedom to its pupils. Now I'm sure of it.'

James sighed, looking down into his empty glass. 'We

47

can hardly blame the school for our daughter's promiscuity,' he stated heavily.

'She certainly does not get her ideas from me, James,' his wife retorted sharply, apparently forgetting for a moment that they were not alone. Then she turned apologetic eyes on Caroline. 'Oh, my dear, what must you be thinking of us? I assure you, Laura is not normally so objectionable.'

Caroline made a deprecating gesture. 'Oh, please, don't mind me. I am aware of the problems parents can have with teenagers today.'

'Are you?' Deborah's eyes were suddenly assessing. 'Yes, I suppose you must be. With your background.' That was subtly done, but Caroline ignored it. 'Laura's led such a – sheltered existence up until now. You've no idea how distressed it makes me feel to think that this – this man has actually laid hands upon her...'

'For God's sake, Deborah, leave it!' James slammed his empty glass down on the tray. 'Excuse me, both of you. I'll go and see how much longer dinner's going to be.'

'Oh, but—' Caroline got awkwardly to her feet as he reached the door. 'I mean – I can eat in my room.'

'Why should you wish to do that?' James's appraisal was no longer inscrutable, but cold and demanding. 'Relax. The cabaret's over for this evening. You will find that even we eat with knives and forks like everybody else.'

Caroline almost shrank from that harsh denouncement, and Deborah exclaimed: 'Darling, don't make the situation any worse for Miss Douglas. I'm sure she was only trying to be tactful.'

'I'm really wondering if there's any point in my staying here,' Caroline got out evenly. 'If Laura—'

'Laura will do as she's told,' said Deborah firmly, dashing any hopes Caroline might have had of making her departure gracefully. 'We, Laura's parents, employed you, Miss Douglas. We will discharge you when your presence here has accomplished its purpose. Do I make myself clear?'

'Yes, Mrs. Booth.'

Caroline took a deep breath, and with a brief glance at both of them, James left the room.

CHAPTER FOUR

DINNER was the most uncomfortable meal that Caroline could ever remember having. Not that she ate a lot, even though the food offered to her was expertly cooked and appetizingly served. An iced consommé was followed by prawns served in a cream sauce, and the main course was lamb cutlets on a bed of baby carrots, peas and beans, with tiny new potatoes cooked in butter. There was a strawberry gateau to finish, which they all refused, and Deborah suggested that she and Caroline adjourn to the lounge for coffee. They left James at the table, helping himself to more wine to drink with the cheese and biscuits he had accepted.

To Caroline, the whole evening had become slightly unreal, and she was glad that the Frobishers were announced just as Deborah was pouring the coffee. Perhaps now she could make her excuses and leave them before James reappeared.

But Deborah would not allow her to get away so easily. When Irene Frobisher and her husband came into the room, she said: 'You're just in time to have coffee with us. David, come and meet the young lady your wife chose for us.'

Caroline forced a smile as she recognized the woman who had interviewed her in London. Irene Frobisher was a few years older than Deborah Booth, and although well corseted was inclined to plumpness. Her husband on the other hand was quite thin, not so tall as James, with greying brown hair and lively blue eyes behind horn-rimmed spectacles.

'Hello again, Miss Douglas.' Irene was coolly polite. 'How are you settling in at Maitlands?'

'Oh, my dear, the girl's had a veritable baptism of fire!'

exclaimed Deborah, rather dramatically, Caroline thought. 'There's been another scene with Laura. James had to send her to her room.'

'Poor old Laura,' remarked David Frobisher tolerantly, giving Caroline an almost conspiratorial grin. 'What has she done now?'

'It's no joking matter, David,' retorted Deborah, looking annoyed. 'Laura has admitted to – to having relations with this man!'

Irene's shocked exclamations were overridden by James's appearance and his words of taut impatience. 'I don't for one minute think that Laura has had – relations – with Mooney,' he told the company shortly. 'Can't you think of anything else to talk about?'

The argument which might have ensued was prevented by David saying casually: 'As a matter of fact, James, I called in to ask whether you'd fancy crewing for me on Sunday. It's the Pastoral Challenge Cup race and young Carney's gone and sprained his wrist playing tennis.'

The conversation divided at this point, James discussing the race with David, and Deborah and Irene exchanging sympathetic comments. Caroline gulped her coffee and stood up.

'If you'll all excuse me . . . I am – rather tired.'

Deborah looked as though she might object, but before she could say anything James intervened. 'Yes, of course. Good night, Miss Douglas.'

Caroline supposed Deborah and the Frobishers said good night too, but after glimpsing the look of intense weariness in James's eyes, all else defeated her.

To her surprise, she slept extraordinarily well. The bed was superbly comfortable, and although she had never slept between silk sheets before, she found it a pleasurable experience. A change, too, from the rather lumpy continental-style quilt which had been all her landlady had provided. She awoke to the sound of birds arguing noisily in the garden outside her windows, and lay for several minutes just savouring the sense of well-being that produced, so different from the roar of traffic which had been all she could hear in London. She leaned over and looked at her watch, lying on the table beside the bed. It was not yet eight o'clock, and she relaxed.

The night before tiredness had overwhelmed her, a kind of mental as well as physical exhaustion which the strain on her nerves had provoked. But this morning her mind was rested and alert, and the events of the previous day could be viewed with more perspective. To her astonishment, she found herself actually contemplating the task ahead of her with some enthusiasm.

But what of other complications? Her brows drew together in an uneasy frown. Was it really possible that until yesterday James had not known of her identity? That until he met and spoke with Mrs. Frobisher he had not associated the governess who had been employed for his daughter with the girl he had once ...

Caroline pushed back the covers and got out of bed. The sun was already glinting through her curtains, and she drew them back, confident that no one could overlook her here. Then she drew back aghast. A man was walking towards the house, a dark man in a dark towelling robe, his hair sparkling with specks of water. As she drew back her curtains, the action must have attracted his attention, because he looked up and saw her, her slender body silhouetted within the drift of chiffon she wore as a nightgown.

Caroline sank back against the bedroom wall, her arms wrapped protectively about herself. Deborah Booth had said that her husband often used the swimming pool in the grounds. Obviously James had been swimming, but what twist of fate had devised that she should draw back her curtains at precisely that moment? She found she was shivering and went swiftly into the bathroom to take a shower. As she pulled the plastic shower cap over her hair she wondered how she could possibly have contemplated staying here longer than was absolutely necessary.

By the time she was dressed, businesslike in a plain navy suit which unconsciously drew attention to her extreme fairness, she had herself in control again, and could almost chide herself for behaving so self-consciously. Seeing her employer, for that was what he was, after all, returning from a morning's dip in his pool should not arouse any emotion inside her whatsoever. It was nothing to do with her, and James could certainly not be blamed for her drawing back her curtains at that particular moment. In future, she would check before acting so impulsively. *In future* . . .

She stopped in the act of fastening her watch about her wrist and examined what those words might mean. Had she decided to stay here after all? Had all yesterday's anger and indignation been for nothing? Or had practical necessity finally won over emotional irrationality? If she was prepared to stay here, she would have to accept two things. First, that James's astonishment when he saw her was genuine, and secondly, that she would be living in the house of a man with little respect for any member of her sex, including his own wife. Could she believe that look of disbelief James had shown in those first revealing moments in this very room? And could she bear to stand by and watch him deceive his wife?

She sighed, and finished fastening her watch. Why should she want to stay? Even if James chose to behave as if he had never passed more than the time of day with her, he would always be there, and she would always be conscious of him. Deborah Booth seemed friendly enough, but Caroline was sufficiently conversant with human nature to know that things might not always be so affable. The house and its appointments were luxurious, but Caroline had never had a sybaritic nature. That was why she had gone to Sri Lanka – the austere life there had appealed to her. And perhaps she had rushed into this job because of her need to get away from Tim. So what was it that appealed to her about it?

The answer came in one word – Laura. Her pupil. The girl she had come here to teach, and in fact the reason for her employment. She would not be an easy charge, and there would be problems beyond the normal range of a teacher-pupil relationship. But she presented a challenge, and more than that, Caroline wanted to help her. Something in the girl was crying out for assistance and understanding, something that defied Caroline to turn her back and walk away because of things that should have been long buried.

A knock at her door halted her self-examination, and she went to open it, still apprehensive of unexpected callers. But it was only the maid, Jenny, who waited outside, a loaded tray in her hands.

'Your breakfast, miss,' she announced shortly. 'Shall I set it out for you?'

'Oh, no, I can do it.' Caroline took the tray, with a smile, aware that her position in the household was as nebulous as a governess had ever been. Neither family nor staff, and often resented by the latter. 'It smells delicious, thank you.'

Jenny nodded indifferently. 'Miss Laura will join you in the library downstairs at nine o'clock,' she added, turning away.

Caroline closed the door and carried the tray to the table in the window. Fruit juice and cereal, grilled bacon, eggs and sausage, toast, marmalade, and coffee. To someone used to a hastily brewed cup of tea and indifferently prepared toast, it was luxury indeed, but Caroline's stomach was not equipped to absorb such a meal. She drank the fruit juice, ate two halves of toast, and swallowed several cups of excellent coffee. The mixed grill congealed on its plate, and she sighed. The hill workers in the tea estates above Kandy could have fed a family for a day on less.

She carried her tray downstairs at five to nine and encountered Mrs. French just coming out of what she later discovered to be the morning room. The housekeeper hastened forward and took the tray from her, saying: 'There was no need for that, Miss Douglas. Jenny could have brought the tray down when she made your bed.'

'I made the bed, actually,' replied Caroline, with a sigh. 'I'm quite prepared to look after my own room. I'm used to it.'

'That won't be necessary, Miss Douglas, and I'd be glad if you'd leave it to us. Jenny has her job to do as well, you know.'

Caroline controlled the retort that sprang to her lips and shrugged her shoulders. 'As you wish, Mrs. French.'

Leaving the housekeeper, Caroline crossed the hall to the library. Hesitating, she knocked, but receiving no reply after a second attempt, she opened the door and looked into the room.

Laura Booth was lounging in a chair at a table which had not been in evidence the night before. She was slouched over the table, her head resting on one hand, staring broodingly into space. She scarcely looked up when Caroline came into the room, and barely responded to Caroline's: 'Good morning.' She was uniformly attired in the jeans and tee-shirt she had been wearing when Caroline first met her, and her straight dark hair was pulled back with an elastic band.

Caroline closed the door and approached the table slowly. Laura looked up at her then, and as though slightly ashamed of her behaviour, pulled her arms off the table and sat upright in her chair.

'Now then.' Caroline was slightly encouraged by this concession. 'I suggest we begin by getting to know one another first, don't you?'

Laura shrugged. 'I should have thought you'd know all about me by now.'

'No. No. I know very little about you, Laura.'

Laura looked sceptical. 'What? With my mother telling everyone I sleep around?'

Caroline shook her head. 'I suggest we try and forget what happened yesterday and begin again.'

Laura lay back in her chair, regarding the other girl through narrowed eyes. She looked amazingly like her father, on guard as she was, that Caroline felt a momentary stab of pain. Then Laura spoke and the image vanished.

'I told you yesterday – you're wasting your time with me, Miss Douglas. They may be able to confine me physically, but mentally they don't stand a chance!'

Caroline pulled out a chair and sat down. 'And that's your final word?'

'Yes.'

'I see.' Caroline rested her elbows on the table, cupping her chin in her hands. 'All right. Suppose you tell me what your plans for the future are.'

Laura frowned. 'Why should I do that? You're not interested in me.'

'How do you know?'

Laura hunched her shoulders. 'I don't have to explain. You're exactly the same as they are. I'm through with explaining.'

Caroline sighed. 'Don't you think you're the one who's jumping to conclusions? Last night you came to my room and tried to persuade me to give in my notice all on the strength of this infatuation for a man—'

'It's not infatuation!'

Caroline's deliberate use of that word had stung the younger girl as she had known it would, and now she had all Laura's attention.

'Well – whatever,' she went on. 'We had never met, we had never even been introduced, and you came to me with some story about being in love with a man whose apparent glamour for you is the fact that he comes from a different walk of life, and expected me to take your side without being in possession of any of the facts!'

'I had hoped, you being – well, not middle-aged – you'd try and understand.'

'Understand? Understand what? What is there to understand? You're attracted to a man of whom your parents do not approve—'

'They've never even met him!'

'—and for this you're prepared to throw up your chances of gaining a decent education!'

'I've been educated. I'm sixteen. I've got seven "O" levels, and lots of girls are working by the time they're my age.'

'I know it. There have to be shop assistants and factory workers, even clerks and bank tellers; but is that the height of your ambition?'

'I don't know what you mean.'

'Doesn't it ever occur to you that lots of these girls who are already earning a living would prefer to go on and gain further education, would jump at the chance of a place at university, and an interesting career ahead of them?'

'That's their problem.'

'I see. So you feel you've had enough of academic studies?'

'That's right.'

'So what are you going to do?'

Laura grimaced. 'What can I do? Wait until I'm old enough to do as I like, I suppose.'

'And what you would like to do is marry this Irish engineer you've been telling me about?'

Laura's expression softened. 'Would I ever?'

'And you see yourself as his wife—'

'Mmm.'

'—and the mother of his children?'

'Mmm, mmm!'

'Isn't that rather old-fashioned?' There was just the right amount of scorn in Caroline's voice and Laura looked at her sharply.

'What are you suggesting? That we should *live* together?'

'Why not?' Now it was Caroline's turn to relax in her chair. 'Why do you feel marriage is necessary?'

'My God!' Laura stared at her aghast. 'If my mother – or my father – could hear you now!' She almost giggled. 'The governess is an anarchist!'

'Not necessarily.' Caroline shook her head. 'It seems to me to be the most sensible solution, in the circumstances.'

'What do you mean – in the circumstances?' Laura looked suspicious.

'Well – your parents don't want you to marry this man, and as you've already anticipated your marriage vows, why not go on doing so? Why make such a fuss about something that's only a formality, after all?'

Laura's face turned a deep red. 'You realize if I go and tell my mother what you've just said, she'll have you thrown out of here?'

'Why should you worry? It's what you want, isn't it?'

'Don't you care?'

Caroline shrugged. 'If I don't have anyone to teach, I might as well go.'

Laura pursed her lips. 'I don't understand you.'

'Why not? I should have thought I was only putting into words your own feelings in the matter.'

'They're not my feelings,' the girl muttered sulkily.

'They're not?' Caroline raised her eyebrows.

'No.' Laura was obviously struggling within herself and finally she said: 'I haven't actually – that is, Johnny hasn't made love to me. Not properly. I – I wouldn't let him.'

'Did he ask you to?'

Laura hesitated. 'Only once.'

Caroline breathed a sigh of relief. So far the gamble was working. 'And why did you refuse?'

Laura sniffed. 'I don't know. I suppose I was afraid. If

I got pregnant, I think Daddy would kill me.' She paused, and then she went on more aggressively: 'But that doesn't mean that I won't ever – I'm not a prude, you know.'

'I never thought you were.' Caroline rested her palms on the table in front of her. 'So – if I am prepared to accept that your feelings for this man are genuine, will you listen to what I have to say?'

Laura looked doubtful. 'Such as what?'

'Well, suppose when you're eighteen you marry this man, Johnny. Suppose there were no objections from your parents, but once you were married you and Johnny were on your own—'

'That's what we want. Johnny doesn't want any of my money!'

'All right. So you and Johnny are married. Where are you going to live?'

'Johnny has a caravan. He tows it around from site to site.'

Caroline hid her dismay. 'And you'd be prepared to live in a caravan?'

'Of course. Why not? Other wives do.'

'Mmm.' Caroline digested this. 'So – do you have any idea of the kind of income an engineer has?'

'Yes. Johnny told me.'

'And do you realize that what Johnny earns in a year, your father probably spends on drinks and tobacco?'

Laura shrugged nonchalantly. 'I don't expect us to be as well off as Mummy and Daddy.'

'That's just as well, because you're not going to be. Nowhere near!' Caroline brought herself up short. She was getting a little too vehement about this. 'Anyway, suppose something happened, suppose Johnny became ill or lost his job. What could you live on? And what if by then you've got a baby to look after?'

Laura wrinkled her nose. 'Stop being so pessimistic! We'd have to be jolly unlucky!'

'But people are, aren't they? Accidents happen, particularly on building sites.'

'Oh, all right, all right. What's your point?'

'My point is that if it was up to you to get a job and earn some money, what could you do? How would you support a family?'

'We'd manage.' Laura was sullen.

'You'd manage a whole lot better if you had a decent career to turn to, something like teaching, for example. Something that isn't consequent upon the economic state of the country.'

Laura rested her chin on her fists. 'I wondered how long it would take you to justify your position here!' she muttered derisively.

'But you can't deny the truth of what I say, can you?'

'Becoming a teacher takes time. I'd have to go to college.'

'I know.'

'You're condemning me to another five years of education!'

'What's five years in a lifetime? Besides, if you had a few "A" levels, there are other careers open to you that don't require a college backing. Radio-therapy, for instance, or nursing. Useful, satisfying occupations that are always in demand.'

Laura breathed deeply, staring down at the table. 'I used to be interested in journalism,' she admitted slowly.

'There you are, then. That's something you could think about.'

'But why couldn't they have allowed me to stay on at Boscombe? I was happy there.'

Caroline hesitated. Then she said quietly: 'I think they were right to take you away.' She ignored Laura's protest, and went on: 'They took you away from temptation. Can you deny it's harder to meet Johnny here than it was at Boscombe?'

'No, of course not. *They* won't allow it.'

'Even so, you admitted he once wanted to make love to

you. Don't you think that would have happened again? Could you be sure you wouldn't give in?'

Laura tossed her head angrily. 'I have to make my own decisions. It's my life!'

Caroline shrugged, folding her hands together. 'All right then, go ahead. Run away with your Irishman. I won't try to stop you. But don't be too disappointed if he turns you away after he gets bored with your immaturity.'

Laura's lips quivered. 'You enjoyed saying that, didn't you?'

'I'm not enjoying any of this, Laura,' Caroline retorted, her patience snapping. 'I'm employed as a governess, not a psychologist! I could go to your mother and tell her you're being obstructive and let her deal with you! But I haven't. I've listened to you bemoaning a fate that most girls of your age would give their right arm for, but I've had it. Right up to here!'

She rose to her feet, anger and impatience uppermost in her emotions and looked down into Laura's strained anxious features. Immediately, she could see James again, and curiously enough, all the anger went out of her.

'Oh, Laura!' she exclaimed frustratedly. 'I'm not your enemy, I'm your friend! If only you'd have the sense to see it.'

Laura's chin wobbled. 'I don't have any friends in this house.'

'You do now.' Caroline sat down again, with a bump. 'Well? What are you going to do?'

Laura heaved a deep sigh. 'If – and it's only if – if I should decide to go on with my studies, would you help me to see Johnny sometimes?'

Caroline was taken aback, but she managed to hide it. She swallowed rather convulsively and said at last: 'If you work hard, if you prove to me that you're serious about this, I'll elect to mediate on your behalf.'

Laura was silent for a few moments, and then she said:

'And if they don't agree?'

'Don't call your parents "they". As if there were two sides in this. Everyone just wants the best for you. As to some disagreement, I'm prepared to stake my reputation on there being none.'

'You don't know my mother!'

Caroline squared her shoulders. 'I don't know your father either,' she said shortly. 'But that's beside the point.'

'You did know Daddy, though, didn't you?' Laura pointed out reflectively.

'I taught the sons of some friends of his father's in the holidays several summers ago,' Caroline replied briefly.

Laura studied her thoughtfully. 'But he called you Caroline, didn't he?' she suggested, as if the realization had just come to her. 'Did you know him well?'

Caroline managed to control her colour with a supreme effort of will power. 'Of course not. I only met him a couple of times.'

'It was funny how he remembered your name right away like that, wasn't it? *Caroline!*' She said the name in a faithful imitation of James's tone. 'Sort of – agonized, wasn't it?' She watched Caroline carefully. 'As if you were the last person he wanted to see.'

Caroline managed a faint smile at this, although the girl's words disturbed her in a curious way. 'You're imagining things, Laura,' she told her lightly. 'Now, do we have a deal?'

Laura sighed once more. 'Maybe. Maybe not. Perhaps we should have a trial period and see how it goes.'

'I'm prepared to agree to that.'

Laura sniffed. 'Why not? You've got nothing to lose.'

CHAPTER FIVE

CAROLINE came out of the Coach and Horses, and looked up and down Fenbourne's quiet main street. At this hour of the afternoon there were few people about, and the warmth of the day cast a watery mirage of shimmering light. The lingering taste of the lager and lime she had just consumed in the tiny lounge bar made her put out her tongue to lick the last remaining drops from her lips, and she sighed almost contentedly. She was having an unexpected day off. Deborah Booth had driven away to London that morning, dropping Laura off at her grandparents' house on the way, and Caroline had decided walk into the village and sample the menu at the Coach and Horses which Groom had recommended.

Unbelievably it was almost two weeks since she had arrived at Maitlands, unbelievable too that she should be able to live in a house with three other people and yet see so little of them. She saw Laura, of course. She was quite satisfied with the progress she was making with her. But of the other members of the household she saw next to nothing. Occasionally, Deborah Booth would appear half-way through the morning session, and join them for their mid-morning break, but apart from this they all led separate lives.

Caroline always had breakfast in her room. Jenny usually brought it up for her, and after that first morning became a little more approachable. Perhaps Caroline making her own bed had had something to do with it, or maybe it was simply that she had realized that Caroline felt no feeling of superiority over the other members of the staff.

A light lunch was served to Caroline and her charge in the morning room, one of the smaller apartments in the house, and although Deborah Booth must eat lunch too, she never joined them. Dinner, after that first evening, was always served in Caroline's room, and this meant that she had no contact with James Booth whatsoever. For this she was relieved.

Over the week-end that Caroline had already spent at the house, when lessons were suspended, all meals were served to her in her room, and she had decided that in future she must make some arrangement to go out at this time or she would feel stifled.

She was still standing enjoying the sun on her bare arms when a car appeared out of the heat haze that shrouded the village street and swept to a halt outside the public house. It was a sleek dark green vehicle, with lines built for speed as well as comfort. It was a car Caroline had seen before, parked outside Maitlands, and panic set her legs in motion.

'Miss Douglas!'

Two men were climbing out of the car, one of them lean and dark, dressed more casually than she was used to seeing him in close-fitting jeans and a half open denim shirt. The other man was similarly attired, around the same height, but with reddish-coloured hair and a drooping moustache.

James's greeting automatically halted her, and she turned to face the two men with extreme reluctance, conscious that for coolness she was wearing little more than thin jeans and a sleeveless vest, her hair secured in a knot on top of her head, with tendrils drifting about her ears and nape. Hardly the attire of a governess, she thought wryly, but then today she was not working.

'Good afternoon, Mr. Booth,' she responded politely, her expression cool and disinterested. She was aware that his companion was regarding her with speculative attention, and a certain cynicism invaded her eyes. It was a situation she had experienced before, she reflected bitterly. The governess attracting the lustful pursuits of a friend of the family! It was almost amusing, and did not trouble her one bit. There were few situations with men she felt she could not now handle.

James glanced about him, frowning. 'Where is Groom? I presume he drove you down to the village,' he suggested.

'No. Groom has driven your wife to town. I walked.'

'With Laura?'

'No. Laura is spending the day with your parents, I believe.'

James's frown deepened. 'You walked – along those country roads! You could have been molested!'

'But I wasn't.'

Caroline realized her remarks to James were hardly in keeping with her image as an employee, but she couldn't help it. That he should be concerned that she might be molested! It was laughable.

'Well, we'll take you back,' announced James shortly, glancing briefly at his companion. 'Oh, Clive, this is – Miss Douglas, Laura's governess.' He paused, and looked again at Caroline. 'Clive Lester.'

'How do you do, Miss Douglas?' Clive Lester insisted on shaking hands. 'We're just about to slake our thirst in the bar here. Won't you join us?'

'Oh, no, thank you—'

'Why not?' Clive arched his brows. 'Isn't it ethical for governesses to take drinks with their employers? Very well, then, I'll buy the round. How's that?'

'I expect Miss Douglas has some shopping to do before she goes back to the house,' suggested James briefly, but it was this dismissal and not Clive's invitation which aroused some demon of wilfulness inside Caroline.

'No,' she said carefully, 'I don't have any shopping to do.' She looked up at Clive through her lashes. 'And if – Mr. Booth doesn't mind, I'd love to join you for a drink, Mr. Lester.'

She heard James's swiftly indrawn breath, but fortunately Clive seemed unaware of anything but his apparent good luck. 'Come along inside, then,' he urged, and with a faint squaring of her shoulders, Caroline led the way back into the pub.

The bar was almost empty, and Clive saw Caroline on to one of the tall stools beside the counter before sliding on to the one beside her. James remained standing, and Caroline would have had to have been made of stone not to be aware of his displeasure. But she refused to allow him to disconcert her. Clive had invited her for this drink, he was paying for it, and if James didn't like it there was nothing he could do. He had no control over her free time.

'We've been sailing,' Clive told her after swallowing half the beer in his glass. 'On the river at Hawlock. Have you ever done any sailing, Miss Douglas?'

'Once,' said Caroline, her gaze shifting to James who was standing with his back against the bar, staring broodingly into space. 'I had a – friend, who had a boat. We went out a couple of times.'

Clive nodded. 'And did you enjoy it?'

Caroline shrugged. 'It was all right. I suppose like everything else, it depends who you're sailing with.'

Clive chuckled, but looking down into her lager, Caroline could almost feel the antagonism emanating from the man beyond him.

'Well, I've never known a woman yet who made a good crew,' said Clive, shaking his head.

'Doesn't your wife crew for you?' suggested Caroline, deliberately, and Clive laughed again.

'My wife? I don't have a wife, Miss Douglas. Oh, I had once, but like your experiences with sailing, I wasn't impressed.'

Caroline stroked a finger round the rim of her glass. 'I see.'

'Not that I'm saying I'm a confirmed bachelor these days,' Clive went on, his eyes challenging hers. 'Just that

I've not met another woman I've wanted to take on – or who's wanted to take me on,' he added modestly.

Caroline decided they had gone far enough in that direction, and changed the subject. 'How nice to be able to go sailing whenever you feel like it!'

Clive grimaced. 'We don't all finish at five o'clock, you know.'

'Oh, you do have a job, then?' Caroline countered mockingly, and he grinned.

'Sure thing. I'm in exporting. You know, earning dollars for Britain's trade deficit. I may act like a butterfly, but I'm very definitely a bee.'

'Can I have that in writing, Clive?' inquired James, speaking almost against his will, but with a throbbing note of suppressed amusement in his voice, and Clive punched him good-naturedly.

'I thought you'd taken an oath of silence, man,' he countered, raising his glass to empty it. 'Are you having another?'

'Not for me, thanks,' replied James, finishing his beer and wiping his mouth with the back of his hand, and Caroline quickly drank her lager.

'That was delicious, thank you,' she assured Clive, as they all walked out into the sunlight again, and James strode ahead to unlock the doors of the car.

Caroline got into James's car with some misgivings, but short of being downright rude, there was nothing she could do about it. She got into the back, and the two men climbed into the front, and then the powerful engine roared to life.

The windows of the car were open as they drove along, and the wind soon loosened Caroline's hair from its knot and had it tumbling about her shoulders. It blew about her face, and into her mouth, and she was wiping it away when she encountered James's eyes on her through the rear-view mirror. Immediately, she looked away, refusing to be intimidated by the coldness of his stare.

The gates of Maitlands loomed ahead, but to Caroline's surprise the car swept past. Clive looked surprised, too, and James said: 'I might as well drop you off first, Clive. I can't stay. I have some work to do at the house. Give my apologies to your mother, won't you?'

Clive Lester apparently only lived a short distance further on, his home an elegant Georgian house with a pillared portico and curved fanlight. When the car drew to a halt on the semi-circle of the drive, he leaned on the window for a moment after climbing out.

'Okay, old man,' he said amiably. 'I'll see you on Sunday evening anyway. Deborah's asked me to dinner.'

'Has she?' James frowned for a moment. 'I didn't know. All right, Clive, see you Sunday, then.'

'Yes.' Clive's eyes shifted to Caroline's windswept appearance. 'Good-bye, Miss Douglas. It's been a pleasure.'

Caroline managed a smile, and then sensing James's impatience, Clive straightened and the car moved away.

Caroline fully expected James to say something as soon as they were out of earshot, but he didn't open his mouth. He concentrated his whole attention on his driving, and within minutes he was sounding his horn for the lodge-keeper to open the gates of Maitlands. Then the car crunched up the drive and slewed to a halt before the front terrace.

Caroline managed to open the door and scramble out before James could come round to help her, and they mounted the terrace steps together. As usual, the doors stood wide, and Caroline preceded him into the hall, not without some relief. But it was short-lived.

'Come with me to my study, please,' he said formally, signifying to the housekeeper who had appeared at their entrance that she was not needed, and Caroline had no choice but to obey.

She had never been in his study before. It was situated down a narrow passage towards the back of the house, and was the one room which Laura had told her was barred, even to her. Caroline only knew that sometimes James came home and worked there, but she had seen so little of him since her arrival that she had hardly known when he was in the house and when he was not.

Now she followed him into his study rather defiantly, hardly noticing the attractive appointments – the matt brown carpet, the hide-covered chairs and leather-topped desk, the long red curtains at the tall windows. She moved to stand beside the desk, unconsciously bracing herself with her fingers against its edge, her eyes sharp and unrepentant.

James closed the door, leaning back against it for a moment, before straightening to move into the room. In the casual clothes he was wearing he looked younger, but there was a look of strain about his lean features. Watching him, albeit surreptitiously, memories of the way he had pursued her all those summers ago returned to haunt her. It was all too easy to recall the persistence with which he had sought her out, talking with her, eating with her, teasing her about her dreams and ideals. They had both known it could only be a matter of time before he made love to her, and the occasions when she had been in his arms had acquired a bitter-sweet anticipation. He was the only man she had ever shared any feeling of intimacy with, and because of him, no man since had been allowed close enough to try. It had taken some time, several months in fact, before she had realized that he had no intention of divorcing his wife and marrying her. It had all come out that awful Friday night in that small motel room, when she had imagined he had left Deborah for good, and all he had planned was a crafty week-end ...

Now he came to stand beside the desk too, and looking down at her, he said: 'Don't ever do that to me again!' in a low angry tone.

Caroline forced a nonchalance she was far from feeling. 'Do what – *Mr.* Booth?'

His hands clenched by his sides. 'You know what I

mean.' A pulse was jerking near his jawline. 'Clive Lester is a friend of mine. Let's keep it that way, shall we?'

Caroline's eyes widened with assumed mockery. 'How could I do otherwise, Mr. Booth?'

'Stop calling me *Mr.* Booth!' he muttered savagely, and half turned away from her.

'What would you have me call you?' she asked, in an undertone. '*James?* I hardly think your wife would approve.'

He hunched his shoulders in a gesture of defeat. 'I think it's time we had this out, don't you?'

Caroline stiffened her back. 'What, precisely?'

'Don't give me that, Caroline. Did you do this deliberately? Coming here, I mean?'

'No, I did not,' she retorted shortly. 'Your friend Mrs. Frobisher employed me—'

'Irene Frobisher is not *my* friend!' he contradicted her.

'All right, your wife's friend, then. So far as I knew, I was being employed by them, for their daughter. How was I to know *your* wife was behind it?'

James drew a deep breath. 'I see. I guessed as much, of course.'

'How well you might!' Caroline's eyes sparkled angrily. 'I wouldn't have accepted a position in *your* household!'

James let this go with only a slight tightening of his lips. 'But you stayed,' he stated bleakly.

'Yes. I hadn't much choice. I'd spent half the advance Mrs. Frobisher had given me.'

James turned to scowl at her. 'If you'd been that desperate, you could have asked me,' he muttered.

'Oh, yes? And if I'd asked you, what would you have done? Given me the money to refund your wife? And how would you have expected payment, I wonder?'

James stared at her bitterly. 'You bitch!' he said harshly, and for once Caroline was ashamed.

'I'm sorry,' she apologized reluctantly, suddenly feeling rather childish. 'It's just – well, you made me angry.'

She looked unwillingly up at him, aware of his nearness as she had not been before. Her eyes were drawn to the opened vee of his shirt, and the brown expanse of chest revealed with its light covering of dark hair. When he had taken her sailing he had worn nothing but a pair of swimming shorts, and when he had pulled her into his arms and unfastened the bra of her bikini . . .

She allowed her thoughts to go no further. It was the climax of that affair she had to remember, not the tantalizing details of a relationship which had rocked the very core of her being.

'Oh, Caroline!' he muttered, in a shaken voice. 'Why for God's sake did you have to come back into my life!'

Caroline moved away, putting the width of the desk between them. 'I haven't come back into your life, James,' she stated steadily. 'I'm here because of your daughter, and nothing else. The fact that we once – knew one another is immaterial.'

'Is it?' His mouth was grim.

'It could be. That was all over six years ago. I've grown up a bit since then. When I first found out – well, I admit my first inclinations were to leave. But after I'd met Laura . . .'

'Yes.' The lines deepened beside his mouth. 'You get on well with Laura.'

'I try.'

'So she told me.' He paused. 'She likes you.'

'Thank you.'

'Don't thank me.' He raked a hand through his hair, allowing his palm to rest against the back of his neck. 'I could wish she disliked you intensely!'

Caroline was shocked at how easily he could still hurt her. 'I'm sorry about that.'

'Are you? Are you really?' Patently, he didn't believe her. 'You don't honestly care what I think about you, do you?'

Caroline held up her head. 'No.'

'So now we know where we stand.'

'If you say so.'

James's hand fell to his side, and he moved to throw himself wearily into one of the soft, hide-covered chairs, one leg draped carelessly over the arm. 'All right, you can go.'

'Yes, *Mr.* Booth, thank you, *Mr.* Booth.'

Caroline didn't know what made her taunt him like that, but when she crossed the room on her way to the door she had to pass his chair, and his hand went out and caught her wrist between hard fingers. 'Don't do it, Caroline,' he warned her, through clenched teeth. 'Don't do it!'

Caroline was not a little frightened by the look in his eyes, but she refused to allow him to see it. 'Don't do what, *Mr.* Booth?'

James sighed, deceptively relaxed, looking at the slim wrist he held with so little effort on his part. 'Knowing you were in the house, Caro, it hasn't been easy,' he told her huskily. 'Whether you believe it or not, you are the only woman I have ever wanted.' Thwarting her efforts to release herself, he went on: 'Don't tempt me to do something you might regret. I'm half-way there already.'

He let her go then, and Caroline snatched her wrist way. 'How – how dare you say such things to me!' she stormed furiously. 'What makes you think I won't go straight to your wife and tell her what a swine you are?'

James shrugged. 'I can't stop you, if that's what you want to do.'

Caroline stared frustratedly at him. 'Don't you care?'

'Let's say, not right at this moment,' he responded, his heavy lids narrowing his eyes.

Caroline turned towards the door, refusing to continue this conversation any further, but his voice arrested her: 'Has there been – *is there* anyone else, Caro?'

She swung round on him. 'You have no right to ask me that!'

'Why not?' There were slumbrous fires burning in the depths of his dark eyes. They reminded her of the excitement she had always felt at being able to arouse this man, almost against his will, she had sometimes thought.

'It's nothing to do with you.'

'Oh, come on, Caroline. You and I were once lovers – oh, not perhaps in the physical sense of the word, but that was merely a lack of opportunity—'

'You flatter yourself!'

'No, I don't. We had something, you and I, and you know it. Okay, you say it's over now. But that doesn't stop me from thinking about you, wondering whether anyone else has got close to that cold little heart of yours!'

Caroline reached for the handle of the door. 'As a matter of fact there have been several relationships,' she told him contemptuously. 'If it interests you to read about them, I'll let you have my diaries. Only don't try to tell me what to do – *Mr.* Booth!'

She had wrenched open the door before he could get up from his chair, but that didn't prevent her heart from pounding giddily, a feeling further increased by the sight of Mrs. French standing right outside. For a moment, she thought the housekeeper had been caught out eavesdropping, but as she fought desperately for control, Mrs. French dispelled this belief in a wave of confusion.

'Oh, Miss Douglas! There's a young man to see you,' she exclaimed, colouring as James appeared behind Caroline. 'He's waiting outside.' Her eyes lifted to James's scowling face. 'Shall I show him in, sir?'

Caroline was aware of James's hostility, and the hand he rested against the door frame close by her ear gave her a suffocating feeling. She wanted to move away from him, but Mrs. French was in front of her, blocking her escape. The only young man Caroline could think of was Tim, but what could he want? And why had he come here?

'Who is it, Mrs. French?' James inquired coldly, and the housekeeper moved her thin shoulders awkwardly.

'It's a Mr. Mooney, sir,' she replied, and Caroline's lips parted in amazement.

'Did you say *Mooney*?' demanded James, the ominous calmness of his tone warning Caroline of his own instant, and unfavourable, recognition of the name.

'Yes, sir.' Caroline could have sworn Mrs. French was enjoying this. 'Will it be all right if I show him into the library, sir?'

James looked down at Caroline, and there was no mistaking the anger in his eyes. 'You were expecting a visitor?' he suggested bleakly.

'No, I was not.' Caroline was indignant. 'I don't know anyone called Mooney!'

'I think you do,' returned James, without emphasis. Then he looked at the housekeeper. 'Very well, Mrs. French. Show Mr. – er – Mooney into the library.'

'Yes, sir.'

The housekeeper went away and Caroline was left staring at her employer. James considered her flushed resentful face closely for several seconds, and then he expelled his breath on a noisy sigh. 'All right,' he muttered harshly, 'what's John Mooney to you?'

'To me?' Caroline gasped. 'I don't even know him. I've told you.'

'You expect me to believe that?' James sneered.

'I don't care what you believe!' she retorted heatedly. 'I don't know John Mooney. I've only heard his name. And I know what you're thinking. But I'm not involved with the man!'

James clenched his fists, thrusting them into the front pockets of his jeans, drawing her unwilling attention to the taut cloth moulding the muscles of his powerful thighs. 'Do you deny inviting him to come here to see you when you expected the rest of the household to be out?' he demanded.

Caroline stared at him incredulously. 'Is that what you think? Is that what you really think?' she asked contemptuously.

James shifted impatiently. 'What else am I expected to think?' he snarled angrily. 'My God, and you let me believe your being here was a coincidence!'

Caroline took a deep breath. She was tempted to march up the stairs, collect her belongings, and leave this house for good. Let them sue her for their money if they wanted, she wouldn't care. But something, some emotion she refused to acknowledge, would not allow her to give in so easily. Whatever happened, he should not spend the rest of his life imagining she had schemed her way in here.

Clenching her nails into her palms, she said: 'Will you listen to me? I did not invite this man – Mooney – here today. I didn't even know I was not going to be working. Your – your wife told me after breakfast that both she and Laura were going out.'

'There are telephones,' retorted James coldly.

'All right, there are telephones. But I didn't use the telephone. Ask Mrs. French. I had lunch in the village.'

'You could have telephoned from there.'

Caroline held her temper in check with difficulty. 'Then why did I come back here? Why didn't I simply arrange to meet him in the village?'

'Because *I* insisted on bringing you home!'

'Oh, yes. And I suppose, knowing you were going to be at home, I hoped that he would come on here if I wasn't waiting for him!' Caroline uttered a scornful exclamation. 'Does that sound logical to you?'

James subjected her to a brooding appraisal. 'Then why is he here? Why has he asked to see you? And how does he know your name? Unless . . . unless . . .'

'Unless,' she prompted him, eyes wide.

'Unless – Laura's at the bottom of this,' muttered James reluctantly.

'Laura!' Caroline expelled her breath on a sigh. 'I didn't think of that.'

'No, nor did I.' James shook his head impatiently. 'God, if she is at the back of this, I'll – I'll—'

'—apologize to me,' suggested Caroline dryly, and he had the decency to colour slightly under his tan.

'Of course.' His lips tightened. 'Naturally, if I have misjudged you . . .' He shrugged his broad shoulders. 'I'd better see him myself.'

'*No!*' Caroline's immediate denial brought a trace of his former suspicion back to his face. 'No, let me,' she pleaded. 'I mean, it was me he asked to see, after all.'

James's brows drew together. 'If this is some trick—'

'Do you think it is?' she challenged him, half angrily.

'God, I don't know what to think,' he muttered, running a questing hand through his hair.

'Oh, *James!*' For a moment, Caroline forgot to maintain the barriers between them, impulsively putting her hand on his arm, feeling the taut muscles beneath her fingers. 'Trust me, James!'

He looked down at her fingers on his arm, and it was as if his flesh became live coals to her touch. Her hand fell away, and she took a step backward, but not before she had glimpsed the torment in his eyes. 'I trust you, Caroline,' he said thickly. 'But don't trust me!' And without another word, he turned back into his study and closed the door.

CHAPTER SIX

Mrs. French was hovering outside the library door when Caroline appeared. 'He's in there,' she said, in a disapproving undertone. 'You watch he doesn't take any of the silver, mind. I don't trust those Irish navvies!'

'He's not an Irish navvy!' Caroline found herself defending him unseen. 'He's Irish, yes, but he's an engineer. Now, if you'll excuse me ...'

She made to open the door and Mrs. French uttered some uncomplimentary epithet as she walked away. Shaking her head, Caroline turned the handle and entered the library.

The young man was standing by the windows, looking out on to the drive at the front of the building, but he turned at her entrance and Caroline saw that he was quite different from her own imaginings. Her imagination, and Laura's unfortunate habit of exaggeration, had created the image of a muscular young giant, proud and aggressive, and totally self-confident.

The reality came as something of a surprise, but not quite a disappointment. John Mooney was a little over medium height, with a lean, bony body, and fairish brown hair which was already beginning to recede, giving the impression of his having a very high forehead. But for all that, he was an attractive man, and Caroline thought she could see why Laura found him so fascinating. There was character in his face, and humour, and a gentleness which even Caroline found disarming.

'Miss Douglas?' he questioned, crossing the room towards her, his well-cut navy suit and crisp white shirt making Caroline more than ever aware of the disadvantages of her own attire. 'How are you?'

Caroline allowed him to shake her hand, and then he

stood expectantly in front of her, putting his hands behind his back. Caroline said: 'How do you do?' and waited also, not quite sure of what her own attitude should be.

This silence between them was uneasy, and suddenly they both broke into speech at the same time. The consequent confusion relieved the situation, and they both laughed. Then, at Caroline's insistence, he said: 'You wanted to see me?'

Caroline gasped. '*I* wanted to see *you*?'

'Well, didn't you?'

'No!' Caroline shook her head in a puzzled way. 'What makes you think I did?'

'I got a message. From you.'

'A message?' Caroline moved her shoulders helplessly. 'How could you? I didn't send any message?'

Mooney stared suspiciously. 'Are you sure?' He frowned. 'Did Laura put you up to this?'

'No. No, of course not.' Caroline was trying to think. 'Please – tell me about this message. Who delivered it?'

'There was a telephone call – at the site.'

'Asking you to come here? to see me?'

'Yes. I didn't altogether understand it myself, but I thought – well, Laura told me you weren't entirely against our friendship.'

'Laura told you that?' Caroline's frown deepened. 'But how could she? She hasn't seen you. Or has she?'

'We speak on the phone occasionally. And write letters. Surely you can't object to that!'

'It's not up to me to object to anything. It's nothing to do with me.' Caroline shifted impatiently. 'Oh, I don't know. Let me think. Could Laura have arranged this meeting, do you suppose?'

He shrugged. 'Don't ask me.' He sighed. 'I hardly think so. The journey's been for nothing, hasn't it?'

'Well, what did you think would come of it? What did you imagine I could do for you?'

'I suppose I thought you might have arranged for me to see her, to spend some time with her. I was obviously wrong.'

Caroline sighed now, aware of a reluctant sympathy for him. 'Well, I'm sorry,' she said. 'But whoever sent you that message, it wasn't me. And Laura's not here. She's spending the day with her grandparents.'

'Oh, great!' He slid his hands into his trousers pockets. 'Well, I suppose I should say I'm sorry to have troubled you.'

Caroline bit her lip. 'That's all right.'

He moved towards the door and then halted. 'I don't suppose . . .' He halted. 'I came on my motor-bike. It's down at the lodge – the old guy who let me in wouldn't let me ride up to the door. I don't suppose you'd consider walking down with me?'

Caroline spread her fingers. 'I don't see why not.' She smiled. 'It's a pity you've come on your motor-bike. We could have walked to the village. I'd like to talk to you – about Laura.'

'Find out what an ignorant peasant I am – is that it?'

Caroline did not flinch. 'If you like.'

He smiled suddenly. 'I could give you a ride on the bike, if you like. I keep a spare helmet in the panniers.'

Caroline hesitated. Walking with him to the village was one thing – going off with him on his motor-bike was quite another. And what would James think?

Then she chided herself angrily. Why should she worry about what James would think? Did he ever worry about what she thought? And besides, it was all quite innocent. If he chose to think otherwise, what could he do about it? This afternoon he had proved how contemptible he could be. How dared he ask her about her private affairs? Had he some idea that she might be prepared to take up with him where they left off?

Realizing that Mooney was waiting for her reply, she said: 'Well – all right. You can take me somewhere we can talk. But not far.'

He nodded. 'Fine. Now, can we walk out of here, or do we have to be released?'

Caroline chuckled. 'We walk. Follow me.'

The drive was not visible from James's study windows, but Caroline was not convinced he was not watching their progress. Or perhaps it was Mrs. French. No doubt she had been detailed to report to her master.

It was years since Caroline had ridden on the back of a motor-bike, not since her student days, but on an afternoon as warm as this it was delightful. The breeze, that had not been evident when they were walking, loosened her hair beneath the helmet, and it was soon wild and tangled, honey gold about her flushed cheeks.

Mooney turned off the road before they reached the village, following a narrow lane which wound beneath an overhanging canopy of trees before giving out on the stretch of turf that edged the river bank. The river bent at this point providing a natural pool, and this spot was completely secluded. The only sounds came from the birds, and the insects humming about the clumps of wild flowers which starred the bank, the movement of water over the stones at its edge providing a cooling background.

Caroline swung her leg over the bike and pulled off her helmet. 'You apparently know this area better than I do,' she commented dryly.

Mooney adjusted the heavy motor-cycle on its stand, and removing his own helmet ran a smoothing hand over his hair. 'I must admit, I know it better than I used to. But Laura showed me this place. She told me she used to come here when she was a kid with her old man. That pool's quite deep. They used to swim.'

Caroline dismissed the image his words unwillingly provoked, wondering what James would say if he could hear himself described in that way. She sank down gracefully on to the grass. 'Well, it's certainly a beautiful place.'

'Mmm, beautiful,' he agreed flinging himself down

beside her, his eyes on the attractive picture she made. 'How come you're a governess?'

Caroline turned to look at him. 'We're not here to talk about me,' she said pointedly.

He lay back, folding his arms behind his head. 'Okay. What do you want to know?'

Caroline sighed, crossing her legs, lotus-fashion. 'I'm not sure I want to *know* anything. I think it just might help if we – well, understood one another.'

His eyes narrowed as he looked up at her. 'Why should you care? You don't approve of me having anything to do with Laura any more than the rest of her family, do you?'

'I – wouldn't say that.'

'Wouldn't you?' He regarded her sceptically.

'No. Look, I'm fond of Laura. She's the only reason I'm here.' She paused. 'You have to admit, you are a lot older than she is. She's still a schoolgirl.'

'And she's a Booth!'

'That, too.'

He sat up, loosening his tie. 'You may not believe this, but I didn't start this. Oh, I'm not saying I held back or anything, but Laura made the running.'

'How did you meet her?' asked Caroline curiously.

He smiled then. 'I guess you could say she picked me up. A group of them used to hang around this coffee bar in Bournemouth. They knew who we were, me and some of the others, and we recognized them because of the uniform, you see?'

'And she wasn't the only one.'

'Hell, no. But – well, I guess our relationship developed into something more serious.'

Caroline shook her head. 'And are you prepared to wait? Until she's eighteen?'

'Wait? Wait for what? To marry her? They'll never let me marry her!'

Caroline was amazed. 'Are you serious?' Her brows drew together. 'Or is this some gambit?'

Mooney took a deep breath. 'It's no gambit. I'm a realist, Miss Douglas. I know Laura thinks she's in love with me, but if her parents succeed in keeping us apart, she'll eventually find somebody else. Somebody suitable, no doubt.'

Caroline gasped. 'Then you don't love her?'

'Oh, I wouldn't say that. No, I wouldn't say that.' He tipped his head on one side, suddenly very Irish. 'I do care about her, I care about her very much. But it would never work. Sure, and haven't I told her that?'

Caroline's shoulders sagged. 'I wish you could have told her father and mother this.'

'What? And put them out of their misery? After the way they've treated Laura? Why should I? Let them worry a while longer. It will do them no harm, and I wouldn't do anything to hurt Laura.'

Caroline laughed. She couldn't help it. The tension she had felt all afternoon was suddenly dispersed like a cloud of smoke, and the day seemed that much brighter.

'Why are you laughing?' he asked goodnaturedly. 'Did I say something funny?'

Caroline shook her head, tugging her fingers through her hair. 'No. No, not really. And thank you – for being honest with me.'

'It was nothing. But you'll not be telling them at the house what I've said?'

Caroline looked thoughtful. 'No, I won't say anything which might get back to Laura. I'd hate to be the one to disillusion her.'

Mooney looked frowningly into the far distance. 'She has a lot of growing up to do.'

'Haven't we all?' commented Caroline, almost inaudibly, and got to her feet. 'Well, shall we go?'

He looked up at her without enthusiasm. 'There's no hurry, is there?'

Caroline sighed. 'Yes. I'd hate to arrive back at Maitlands just as Laura was arriving back from her grandparents' house. What kind of interpretation do you think she'd put on our being out together?'

Mooney got to his feet. 'I might not mind,' he responded quietly. 'What's your name? Caroline? Can I call you that? You know my name. Meet me again, Caroline, when we don't have to spend the time talking about someone else.'

Caroline stepped back aghast. 'I can't do that.'

'Why not?' He frowned again. 'You're not – engaged, are you?'

'Well – no. But—'

'But what?' He wasn't much taller than she was and their eyes were almost on a level. 'Who knows that my involvement with Laura was not just fate's way of devising our meeting?'

'I've heard of blarney, but—'

'It's not blarney, honestly.' His grey eyes were steady and appealing. 'I don't know many girls—'

'I don't believe it!'

'—and I wish you would come out with me. I get lonely sometimes.'

'I can't.' Caroline sighed. 'Besides, what if Laura should find out?'

'She won't.'

'No! No, I can't.' Caroline turned abruptly away. His words were too similar to those James had used when she had protested that his wife might find out. And Laura was James's daughter. She couldn't do it. She wasn't even sure she wanted to. John Mooney was an attractive man, and she couldn't deny that in other circumstances she might have been prepared to go out with him. But this was different.

Realizing she could not be persuaded, John strolled across to his bike and put on his helmet, tossing the other to Caroline. She fastened the straps, and after he had straddled the motor-bike and started the engine, she climbed on the back.

83

'You trust me to take you straight back, then?' he challenged, and she smiled.

'Yes, I trust you. To take me straight back anyway.'

It took only minutes to reach the gates of Maitlands, and Caroline dismounted, not without some relief that they appeared to be unobserved. John was feeling for something inside the jacket of his suit, and presently he produced a small square of white cardboard.

'My card,' he told her, handing it over. 'My telephone number at the site is on there. Should you want to reach me ...'

'Why should I want to do that?' she exclaimed.

'Who knows?' he countered with a grin, and letting out the clutch surged away at a rapidly increasing pace.

Dodds opened one of the drive gates an inch or two to allow her to enter the grounds. He was an elderly man, who lived at the lodge with his wife, and who looked after the lawns and flower beds as well as vetting would-be visitors. His mouth was drawn down disapprovingly as he closed the heavy gate behind her, and he said: 'Miss Laura's been looking for you, miss. Nobody at the house knew where you'd gone!'

'Miss Laura!' Caroline echoed in dismay. 'She's back?'

'Seems like it. Mr. Booth brought her home himself, he did.'

'Mr. – Booth? Oh, you mean the elder Mr. Booth.' Caroline put a hand to her head. 'And did you tell Miss Laura where I'd gone?'

'I said you'd gone out with a young man on a motorbike, miss. I didn't know where you'd gone any more than anybody else.'

'No. No, of course not.' Caroline began to walk up the drive. 'Er – thank you, Mr. Dodds.'

Half-way up the drive, she saw Laura running to meet her, her young face flushed and petulant. 'There you are!' she exclaimed, reaching the older girl. 'Where have you been? And what was Johnny doing here? It was Johnny you went off with, wasn't it?'

'Yes.' Caroline hastened on before Laura could interrupt. 'But I wish you hadn't asked him to come here while you were going to be out. Your father wasn't very pleased.'

'Me?' Laura's pent-up emotions were released in a cry of protest. 'I didn't tell him to come here! What are you talking about?'

'You didn't?' Caroline managed to infuse just the right amount of surprise into her voice. 'I thought you must have done.' It was giving her breathing space, and right now she needed it.

'Why would I do a thing like that?' Laura demanded.

'Well, I suppose I thought – you wanted me to meet him, to appreciate the kind of young man he is.'

'And did you?'

Caroline heaved a sigh. They were approaching the terrace and she could see a sleek cream Rolls parked below the steps. Robert Booth's car, she presumed. And he would recognize her, just as James had done. Oh, God, what a tangled web! But at least he knew nothing about her relationship with James, did he?

'We can't talk now, Laura,' she exclaimed. 'Your grandfather's here, isn't he? Shouldn't you be entertaining him?'

'Daddy's there. We've all been looking for you. Daddy was furious! I don't know why. He should have been pleased that you'd gone off with Johnny. After all, think how delighted they'd all be if you succeeded in taking Johnny away from me!'

'Oh, Laura!' Caroline made a helpless gesture as they mounted the steps to the doors. 'Look, I'll have to go and change.' She indicated her vest and jeans. 'We'll talk later—'

'Where the hell have you been?'

Caroline had been concentrating on Laura and the unexpected words were like a douche of cold water. James confronted them in the hall, legs astride, arms folded, his expression as furious as Laura had led her to believe.

Licking her lips, Caroline dragged her eyes away from his angry face, and examined the reaction this was having on Laura. 'I'm sorry if you thought I'd disappeared, Mr Booth,' she replied, hoping to arouse a conspiratorial support from the girl. 'I thought it would be easier if we talked away from the house.'

'That's right, Daddy,' Laura added slowly, responding to Caroline's silent appeal. 'Miss Douglas has told me all about it.'

James's face looked even grimmer. 'And what was he doing here, Laura? And why did he ask to see – Miss Douglas?'

Laura made an indifferent movement of her shoulders. 'I – er – I asked him to come,' she said at last, and now Caroline's lips parted in dismay. She had not wanted Laura to go this far. Her eyes darted back to James's face, and she was not encouraged by what she saw there.

'What's going on, James?'

Now it was Robert Booth's turn to interrupt them. He stood in the doorway to the lounge, regarding them all with tolerant amusement. A handsome man, in his sixties, Caroline estimated, he was an older edition of his son, but when he saw her his relaxed features stiffened, and a mottled darkness spread up over his skin. His eyes shifted incredulously to his son's, and watching him Caroline knew, without a shadow of a doubt, that Robert Booth had known of their relationship. James seemed unperturbed by his father's reactions, however, and Laura was too upset to recognize the undercurrents here.

'I think – I think it's obvious that Miss Douglas has suffered no ill effects from her outing, James,' his father said now. 'Laura, you had no right to invite that scoundrel here for whatever purpose—'

'He's not a scoundrel,' Caroline felt bound to protest. 'He's – well, he's an educated man. He's not a fortune-hunter or anything like that. He came here because –

well, because he was invited to come. I don't think that's any reason for anyone to get so heated about it!'

'Nor do I,' put in Laura. 'None of you know Johnny. How can you condemn him unseen?'

Caroline saw the way James's jaw hardened as his hands fell to his sides. 'Very well, Laura,' he said coldly. 'As we have Miss Douglas's undoubtedly – experienced opinion to go on, we'll excuse your irresponsible behaviour this time. But in future, Miss Douglas,' his lips twisted contemptuously, 'kindly inform me before you decide to go off with a complete stranger!'

'Yes, *Mr.* Booth.'

The offensiveness of Caroline's acquiescence matched his own, and James turned abruptly away, walking back into the lounge. His departure left an awkward silence, and Robert Booth broke it by saying:

'We've met before, haven't we, Miss Douglas? At the Forsters?'

Caroline swallowed the indignation she felt towards James, and forced a faint smile. 'That's right, Mr. Booth. Six years ago. It's a long time.'

'And now you're working for my son.'

His meaning was unmistakable, and Caroline had to school herself not to blurt out the whole unpalatable truth. Instead, she nodded, and said: 'Small world, isn't it?'

'Indeed.' Robert Booth looked vaguely disconcerted, as though he had not expected so casual a reply. 'If you'll excuse me ...'

He followed his son into the lounge and when the door had closed behind him, Caroline expelled her breath on a noisy sigh. Then, shaking her head, she moved towards the stairs. But Laura came after her.

'Did you mean what you said, Miss Douglas? About – about Johnny being an educated man – and not a fortune-hunter?'

Caroline reluctantly nodded her head. 'Of course.'

'Oh!' Laura pressed her palms to her cheeks, obviously well pleased with this reply. Then as Caroline would have gone on, she added: 'I'm glad you met him. It makes it more real somehow, being able to talk about him with someone who actually knows him. That's one of the things I miss about school – not being able to talk about things with the other girls. We used to discuss our boyfriends, Miss Douglas. Oh, I didn't tell them any of the really personal things Johnny and I used to do together, but you know what I mean...'

This was getting worse and worse. 'I must get changed!' Caroline exclaimed desperately. 'Laura, your mother will be home soon.'

'Oh, yes.' Laura's mouth turned down at the corners. 'I wonder what she'll say when she finds out Johnny's been here?'

Caroline didn't want to speculate. This day which had begun so well had got completely out of hand. First her confrontation with James, then John Mooney's unexpected appearance, and now discovering that Robert Booth had known of her involvement with his son... It was all too much.

'I'll see you later, Laura,' she said, determination sharpening her voice, and Laura was sufficiently enamoured of her own thoughts to let her go without pressing her further about who it was who had summoned Johnny to the house.

But once in the comparative security of her bedroom, Caroline could not dismiss that question. Who had brought Mooney to Maitlands, and for what purpose? If it was not Laura, who else would achieve anything by doing such a thing? Unless... Caroline unfastened the waistband of her jeans and stepped out of them. Unless he had made that up – about someone inviting him here. It was a reasonable solution, and while it didn't quite tie in with what her impression of him had been, nevertheless, it would solve an irritating puzzle. He had said he had heard of her from Laura. He had known her name.

But how had he known that Laura – or her parents, for that matter – would not be in the house? Of course, he had said that he had hoped to see Laura. So perhaps it had been a gambit, after all. An attempt to see Laura, through her. Caroline shook her head. What else could it be?

She walked into her bathroom and turned on the taps, allowing more cold water to escape than hot. There was always the possibility that someone from Boscombe might have devised the idea of surprising Laura. One of her school friends, perhaps? Caroline shook her head. They would probably never find out for certain. And was it that important anyway? She sighed. What was more important was James's behaviour, his apparent disregard for the fact of his father's innocent involvement in all this. What must Robert Booth be thinking of her? She shuddered to consider it. Would James explain? She hoped so. But how could she be sure after his behaviour today that his explanations would not be unbearably biased?

Stripping off her panties, she stepped into the water, revelling in the coolness of it against her heated flesh. She stretched her length, allowing the scented ripples to close over her rose-tipped breasts, submerging herself almost completely, uncaring that her hair was getting soaked in the process. She should never have come here, should never have allowed herself to get involved.

To her astonishment, however, Deborah Booth made no mention of John Mooney's visit when she joined Laura and her governess for coffee the following morning. In truth, Deborah seemed absorbed with her own thoughts, and Caroline thought she looked more strained than usual. But when she commented upon the fact Deborah almost snapped her head off, saying that she was perfectly well and did not respond to polite sympathy.

After she had gone, Laura made a face at Caroline.

'Daddy didn't tell Mummy about Johnny coming here,' she explained, not without some satisfaction. 'I think Grandfather persuaded him not to. It would only have caused more trouble, and there was no harm done, was there?'

Caroline didn't know whether to be glad or sorry. She didn't like the intrigue, but similarly she had not looked forward to explaining her behaviour to Deborah.

'I wish I knew why he came, though,' Laura went on, frowning now. 'Are you sure you didn't ask him to come, Miss Douglas?'

Caroline gasped. 'No! Laura, be sensible! Why should I ask him to come here?'

'I don't know.' Laura rested her elbows on the table, cupping her chin in her hands. 'Oh, I wish I'd been here. I wish I'd seen him!'

Caroline had no answer to this. Instead, she indicated the passage of Milton's which they had been discussing before the break, and to her relief Laura was diverted.

CHAPTER SEVEN

DEBORAH BOOTH sent for Caroline on Saturday morning while she was getting ready to go up to London and surprise Tim. She had been contemplating asking whether anyone would object if she spent the night in town, but Deborah's summons put all such thoughts out of her head. As she ran down the stairs to the morning room, where Jenny had told her her employer was waiting, her thoughts were full of James and Laura, and the visit of John Mooney which she felt sure Deborah had somehow found out about.

But to her amazement, Deborah wanted to ask her to join a small dinner party she was giving the following evening.

'There'll only be eight of us,' she told the girl smilingly. 'James and myself, of course – my in-laws, Mr. and Mrs. Robert Booth – Trevor Frobisher, Mrs. Frobisher's eldest son, who's just returned from two years in South Africa – Laura – Clive Lester, a friend of my husband's – and yourself.'

Caroline wondered whether James had engineered this and sought about desperately for an excuse to be absent. 'I – well, actually, Mrs. Booth, I was hoping to spend the week-end in town,' she explained apologetically.

But Deborah was not so easily put off. 'I hope you aren't going to let me down, Miss Douglas. I'll be honest with you, the young lady who was to have partnered Mr. Lester has been taken ill, and I'm at my wits' end to even the numbers at such short notice.'

Caroline made a sympathetic sound. 'I'm sorry, but—'

'Oh, please. You'll enjoy it. You can't have had much entertainment since you came to us.'

'But, Mrs. Booth—'

'Surely you intended returning here tomorrow evening, Miss Douglas?' Deborah's tones had cooled perceptibly. 'I have no objection to your spending the night in town, if that's what you're suggesting, but is it too much to ask you to come back a little earlier than you might have done and join us for dinner?'

Caroline sighed. Short of being downright rude, what could she say? 'Well—' she began, and Deborah seized on her weakening.

'I knew I could rely on you, Miss Douglas! Very well then, you'll join us for drinks in the library tomorrow evening. Shall we say – seven-thirty?'

'Thank you.'

Caroline had no idea why she thanked her, and later, after Groom had driven her to Reading station and she was travelling up to town in the train, she felt that awful sense of impending disaster which always accompanied the anticipation of something unpleasant. Had James arranged this? Was he responsible for Deborah including her in the numbers? And if so, what exactly did he hope to get out of it?

The prospect of Sunday evening's dinner party spoiled her week-end. To begin with, Tim was delighted to see her. He was a teacher, too, although primarily he had begun his career as a commercial artist. Now, he did some freelancing, but he earned his real living from teaching in a college of further education. He had a flat in Chelsea, and ever since Caroline had known him he had been trying to persuade her to share it with him in whatever capacity suited her best. He had given up asking her to marry him before she left for Sri Lanka, but he never gave up hope that some day she would change her mind.

They had lunch in the Chinese restaurant round the corner from his flat, and she told him all the usual things about her job, except her employer's identity. Once, in a fit of depression, she had confided that unhappy period of her life to Tim, and she dreaded telling him that she was now living in the same house as the man who had hurt her so badly.

It was while he was telling her about one of his students that her mind began to wander, and she came to with a start when he exclaimed: 'Hey! Are you listening to me?'

Caroline apologized at once. 'I'm sorry, Tim. What were you saying?'

'What were you thinking about? That's more to the point.'

Caroline forced a smile. 'Nothing much.'

'Are you sure?' He frowned. 'Now I come to think about it, you are looking rather peaky. Are they working you too hard?'

'Heavens, no!' Caroline could be honest about that. 'I'm enjoying it. Laura's an intelligent girl.'

'Laura? That's the girl you're tutoring?'

'That's right.'

'What's she like? As a person, I mean? One of these hidebound females who considers anyone out of their income bracket should touch their forelock before approaching?'

'Oh, no.' Caroline relaxed. 'Quite the reverse, actually. The reason she's been taken away from school is because of her involvement with an Irish engineer working on the motorway near the school.'

'Hey, is that so?' Tim sounded amused. 'She sounds quite a kid!'

'She is.'

'What's her name again? Frobisher? Laura Frobisher? It doesn't ring any bells.'

'It wouldn't.' Caroline hesitated. 'Actually, her name's – Booth. Laura Booth.'

'Did you say Booth?' Tim's eyes narrowed as they considered her expressive face. 'Say, didn't you once tell me that that fellow you got – well, hung up on, had a daughter?'

'Oh – oh, yes. Yes.' Caroline hunched her shoulders, resting her chin on her balled fist. 'You might as well know. He's my employer.'

'What?' Tim was flabbergasted. Then he assumed a hurt expression. 'You weren't going to tell me, were you?'

'I – perhaps not. But I didn't know myself until I got there, Tim. That Frobisher woman interviewed me, as you know, so how was I to guess that Deborah Booth, being an invalid, avoided that kind of thing?'

'Is that what she told you?'

'Afterwards, yes.'

'So why didn't you refuse to take the job when you found out who it was?'

Caroline sighed. 'I was going to. But – well, I met Laura and I decided to stay.'

'Are you sure that's the only reason?'

'I think so.'

Tim sighed. 'So how did Booth react to your appearance?'

Caroline flushed. 'He guessed what had happened. He knows I want nothing more to do with him.'

'Does he?' Tim looked sceptical. 'Well, well. So you're his daughter's governess! What a twist!'

Caroline looked down at her plate. 'Don't be mad at me, Tim. It's just a job, that's all.'

'Is it? If he's not interested in you any more, how come he didn't just fire you? How does he know you won't go to his wife and tell her about her husband?'

'Surely if he fired me without cause, his wife would have some justification for feeling suspicious,' exclaimed Caroline reasonably.

Tim looked unconvinced. 'What about his wife? What's she like?'

Caroline considered before replying. 'I'm not sure. She seems friendly enough sometimes, and at others . . .' She paused. 'As a matter of fact – she's asked me to join her dinner party tomorrow evening.'

'What?' Tim was astounded. 'You? Why?' His eyes narrowed. 'Are you sure it's *Mrs.* Booth who's issuing the invitation?'

Caroline hunched her shoulders. 'I've asked myself that,' she admitted reluctantly. 'But it must be. James would never—'

'*James?*'

'Oh, Tim! Stop trying to trip me up. Yes – *James*! What would you have me call him? *Mr.* Booth? Tim, I loved him! For three months I – I just lived for him.' She caught her breath. 'Don't expect me to forget that.'

'Oh, Caroline!' Tim grasped her hand across the table, squeezing it tightly. 'Caroline, you're a fool, do you know that? Staying in that house. Whatever you say, you're not indifferent to James Booth, and staying there you're just building up unhappiness for yourself.'

'I'm not!' Caroline snatched her hand away, twisting both hands together in her lap. 'Don't you see, Tim? This is the only way. I can't run away from myself all my life.'

'Is that what you've been doing?'

'Maybe.'

'You're crazy!' Tim glared angrily at her.

'Tim, I've told you, it's a job, that's all. And I'm reasonably good at it, even if I do say so myself. It's the only thing I am any good at.'

'I'd love to prove you wrong about that,' muttered Tim, with a sigh, but he didn't pursue the subject.

Nevertheless, their conversation had soured the weekend, and although Caroline spent the evening at the flat and later occupied Tim's bed while he slept on the couch in the living room, as he had done many times before, it wasn't the same.

On Sunday morning, Caroline awoke heavy-eyed after only a couple of hours' sleep to find Tim still sleeping soundly on the couch. She washed and dressed quietly, and left the flat without waking him, a brief note of explanation propped beside the couch. It was cowardly, but she didn't think she could face any more recriminations.

It was too early to return to Maitlands, and she walked briskly up the Fulham Road towards the park. She intended to deposit her overnight case at the left luggage office at Paddington station, and then find somewhere to have breakfast. But she had only gone a few yards when a low sleek green car drew alongside her.

Caroline stepped back from the kerb in alarm. It was still very early in the morning, and there were few people about. There was something about the car which was familiar, however, and her eyes widened in amazement when James rolled the nearside window down, and said sharply: 'Get in!'

Caroline halted, looking nervously about her. 'I – why?'

James thrust the car door open from inside, and levered his long legs across the consol to get out beside her. His dark green suede pants were creased, he was wearing a thick roll-necked sweater, and there was a covering of stubble on his jawline. His eyes were red-rimmed, and there were lines of fatigue around them.

'Get in, Caroline,' he said insistently, his voice low yet betraying a latent note of violence.

'Where have you come from?' she exclaimed, her eyes darting to his, then away again. 'What are you doing here?'

'Get in and I'll tell you,' he muttered, taking her case from her unresisting fingers. 'Come on! I'm on a yellow line. Do you want me to get a ticket?' He threw her suitcase on to the back seat.

Caroline was tempted to tell him that she didn't particularly care what happened to him, but something in his eyes silenced her. With an indifferent shrug she subsided into the low front seat of the car, and he slammed the door before walking round the bonnet to get in beside her.

The car smelt of stale alcohol and cigar smoke, and she

wrinkled her nose fastidiously. An empty bottle nudged her feet, and looking down she saw that it had once contained Scotch whisky. She turned to stare at James; concentrating on the traffic he could not return her scrutiny, and she felt an awful sense of inevitability causing an actual physical ache in her stomach. What was he doing here? And how had he found her? She didn't like to speculate on the obvious solution.

James turned the car off the main thoroughfare at the next junction, following a maze of small streets which Caroline had scarcely known existed until they came out beside an iron-railed cemetery wall. James looked up and down the street, and then drew the car into the kerb, switching off the engine.

'Shall we walk?' he suggested, and Caroline looked doubtfully at the cemetery. 'At least it's quiet,' he added harshly, and with a sigh she thrust open her door.

A notice announced that in summer the cemetery gates were open from sunrise to sunset, and Caroline walked between the tall iron railings into the deserted graveyard. It was still quite cool and she was glad she was wearing her turquoise jersey jacket over the yellow shirt and slacks she had worn to travel in. James walked beside her, his hands thrust deep into the pockets of his pants, his expression dark and brooding.

'Who is he?' he asked at last, the words taut and bitter between his teeth.

Caroline did not pretend to misunderstand what he meant. 'His name is Timothy Frankland. But I don't see what it has to do with you.'

'Don't you?' James stepped across her path then halting them both. 'Who is he? And how is it you spend the night at his flat?'

'James!' Caroline took a deep breath. 'You have no right to check up on me.'

'Believe it or not, I followed you because I was sure you were going to meet Mooney!'

'*What?*'

'You heard what I said.' James's mouth was a thin line. 'What a fool I was. I should have known you wouldn't be that stupid!'

Caroline's fingers stung across his cheek before she could stop herself, and looking down she saw the way his hands clenched in his pockets. 'I don't have to take that from you, *Mr.* Booth!' she snapped angrily. 'What I do in my own time is my own affair.'

James was breathing deeply, and she knew he was controlling his temper with difficulty. 'And where were you going now? To Boscombe, perhaps?'

Caroline half turned away from him. 'Why should I want to go to Boscombe?'

'That is where Mooney stays, isn't it? Where his caravan is resting?'

'Oh, for goodness' sake!' Her eyes flashed angrily. 'I've told you, I don't know John Mooney any better than you do.'

'Don't you?'

'No.' She made an exasperated gesture. 'Oh, yes, I've spoken with him, haven't I? But you could have done that.'

'*You* wouldn't let me.'

Caroline sighed. 'He asked to see me. I don't think he would have talked to you.'

'If you think I swallowed that garbage about Laura's asking him to speak to you, I didn't!'

Caroline moved her shoulders in a dismissing gesture. 'I can't help that.'

'What I can't understand is Laura's desire to abet you.'

'Oh, James!' Caroline turned back to him, unwillingly distressed by the torment in his face. 'James, you don't have to worry about Laura – honestly. No harm will come to her, believe me!'

He brought his hands out of his pockets then, flexing his fingers against his thighs. 'God help me, Caroline, I didn't spend the night outside Frankland's flat for Laura's sake!'

Caroline caught her breath, stepping back from him, shaking her head slowly from side to side. 'No – no, James,' she protested faintly, as his hands reached for her. 'I – you can't do this—'

His hands closed on the yielding flesh of her upper arms and he propelled her resisting body towards his. 'I have to, Caroline,' he muttered in a tortured voice, 'I have to . . .'

His mouth on her parted lips was hard and passionate, his breathing mingling with hers, filling her with the smell and feel of him. His hands slid exploringly over her back, and although she struggled, her hands were crushed between them, the stubble on his chin rough against her face. She had not realized she would remember the angles of his body so well, or how strong would be the impulse to yield against him and respond to the urgency of his touch. She felt his hands beneath her woollen jacket, separating her shirt from her pants, and then the warmth of his spread fingers against her spine.

'James,' she protested, against his mouth, but he didn't stop, and in that sunlit graveyard there was no living being to intervene.

'Don't fight me, Caro,' he breathed into her mouth, and almost against her will she was kissing him back, her arms sliding round his waist, her mouth moving under his. He shuddered and held her closer, and suddenly she knew that he had no intention of letting her go. In a minute he would draw her down on to the grass between the gravestones, and then . . .

She didn't know whether she had the strength, or the will, to resist him, but one thing was certain, she had to try. Closing her eyes against the undeniable attraction of his sensuality, she lifted her foot and kicked him hard on the shin, taking advantage of his momentary relaxation of his hold on her to put some distance between them. She ran to the cemetery gates, panting as much with emotion as anything, and then stopped short. Her case was in James's car. Her handbag, too, and she hadn't a cent with her to take her back to Maitlands.

Pushing her shirt back into the waistband of her pants, she turned and looked apprehensively behind her. James was walking slowly towards the gates, his head bent, apparently unaware of her presence. Watching him, Caroline wondered why she didn't feel anger or disgust towards him, why she felt this ridiculous sense of – what? Compassion? Sympathy? Why should she feel compassion for a man who deserved her contempt? The answer was simple, of course. *Love conquers all*, she thought cynically, but there was more than a thread of warning in that disturbing realization.

He looked up as he approached her, and adopting a defiance she was far from feeling, she said: 'Can I have my belongings, please?'

James looked at her blankly, and then shrugged his shoulders. 'Why? If you're going back to Maitlands, I'll drive you.'

'I don't want to drive with you. Besides, what would your wife think if we arrived back together? Particularly considering you've spent the night away from home!'

'I don't particularly care,' he told her coldly.

'Well, I do. I don't want to lose my job just because – well, just because of you.'

He shrugged again. 'As you wish.'

Opening the car, he hefted her suitcase out on to the pavement, and then handed her the bag which she had left lying on the seat.

'Thank you.'

Caroline looped her bag over her shoulder and picked up her case. James leaned against the bonnet of the car, but he was not watching her. His expression was controlled and remote, only his eyes betrayed that he was not unmoved by her behaviour. She took a step away from him, and then looked back, a niggling sense of responsibility troubling her conscience.

'James,' she said appealingly, and when he turned to look at her, she hurried on: 'James, I – I didn't sleep with him. Tim, I mean – Tim Frankland. You might not believe this, but I don't. I – I never have.'

His eyes darkened. 'Why are you telling me this?'

She flushed then. 'I don't know. I – I suppose I thought you might – you might be interested.'

'Interested?' He muttered a short mirthless laugh. 'Oh, go away, Caroline. Leave me alone! I wish to God I never had to see you again!'

It was late when Caroline got back to Maitlands. She had done as she had originally intended and deposited her luggage at the station, but instead of finding a coffee bar and having breakfast, she had taken a bus to Southend, and joined the holidaymakers thronging the beach and promenade. She had needed the anonymity of being one of a crowd, and she had known there was little chance of her meeting anyone she knew there.

Consequently it was late when she got back to town, and even later when the Bristol train set her down at Reading. Of course, Groom was not there to meet her, so she took a taxi out to the house, grimacing at the hole the fare made in her remaining cash. If she wasn't careful, she would be spending the following month's allowance and condemning herself to another four weeks here. And right now, she felt sure she should be handing in her notice.

She saw no one but Mrs. French as she made her way to her bedroom, but James's Jensen was parked on the drive, and she wondered at the feeling of relief she experienced knowing that he was safely home. However, she had hardly had time to open her case and take out her sponge bag before someone knocked at her door. She hesitated a moment, and then taking a deep breath, she went to open it, relaxing somewhat when she found

Laura outside.

'Hi!' The girl was reassuringly normal. 'Can I come in?'

Caroline stepped aside and Laura entered the room, swinging round as Caroline closed the door and grinning excitedly. 'You'll never guess what!' she exclaimed. 'I've seen Johnny!'

Caroline sank down weakly on to the side of her bed. 'You have?'

'Yes. Today, in Fenbourne. He rang here. He said he was going to ask for you if anyone else answered, but what with Daddy away sailing for the week-end, and Mummy busy with this dinner party she's giving tonight, I got to answer it myself.'

So that was where James was supposed to have been! Caroline sighed. 'I see,' she said, rather absently, realizing that if James found out about this, he would think the worst. But why should she care? she asked herself. Perhaps it would be as well if he did think she was involved with someone else. So why did she go to such lengths to disabuse him?

'You don't mind, do you?' Laura was asking now, looking at Caroline rather anxiously. 'I mean, it was all quite innocent. We just walked – and talked.'

Caroline lay back on the bed, stretching her arms above her head. 'I don't know, Laura,' she said wearily. 'I don't like the idea of being made scapegoat for your intrigues. You know very well that if your mother finds out, she'll blame me for encouraging you. And who can argue with that?'

'Why should she find out?'

Caroline propped herself up on her elbows. 'Parents always do. Oh, look, I thought we had an arrangement.'

'We did. You said you'd help me to see Johnny sometimes—'

'I said no such thing!'

Laura hunched her shoulders, adopting the same rebellious expression she adopted with her parents. 'You did, too. You said if I worked hard—'

'Laura! I've only been here a little over two weeks! Give it time. How can I help you if you persist in behaving in a way of which your parents can't possibly approve?'

'Why shouldn't I see Johnny occasionally? If we can arrange it?'

'Well, I hope he doesn't expect to make a habit of calling here and asking for me!' Caroline's eyes narrowed as they took in Laura's guilty appearance. 'You haven't arranged that, have you?'

'No!'

Laura's reply was too vehement, and Caroline frowned. 'But you have arranged to see him again,' she stated, with impatience.

Laura pouted her lips. 'I don't see why I should tell you,' she said sulkily.

'You want me to go and tell your mother where you've been today?'

'You wouldn't!'

Caroline sat upright. 'Try me.'

Laura was obviously fighting a losing battle with defiance. 'Oh – oh, all right. Yes. Yes. I've promised to meet him on Friday evening.'

'Laura!' Caroline slid off the bed. 'And I'm expected to be a party to this!'

Laura bent her head. 'You said you were my friend!'

Caroline raised her eyes heavenward. 'I am, I am. But that wasn't the arrangement, was it? Your going ahead and meeting – Johnny secretly isn't going to endear him to your parents, is it?'

'They'll never agree to me meeting him.'

'You don't know that.' Caroline shook her head helplessly. 'I've told you, I'll help. But not like this. And – and if he rings here again, you can tell him what I've said.'

'So when do I see him?'

Caroline paced restlessly about the bedroom. 'Later, Laura, later. In a couple of months—'

'A couple of months!' Laura was horrified.

'These things take time, Laura. Trust me! I do know what I'm talking about.'

But did she? And who was she to advise anyone? She hadn't exactly made a success of her own life, had she?

Laura scuffed her toes dejectedly. 'How do I know you don't have a vested interest in keeping us apart?' she muttered in a low tone.

Caroline's eyes widened. 'What do you mean?'

'Well, Johnny did come here to see you when I was out, didn't he? And he told me that message he received was supposed to be from you. How do I know you're not interested in him yourself?' Maybe if someone else had answered the phone today, he would have asked for you because that was who he really wanted to speak to!'

'Oh, Laura!' Caroline licked her lips. 'Do you honestly think that?'

Laura sniffed miserably. 'I don't know what to think.'

Caroline turned away, pressing her palms to her cheeks. 'Well, whether you believe this or not, I had never seen John Mooney before he came to the house that day. And contrary to your suspicions, I am not attracted to him!'

Laura sighed, her lower lip trembling. 'That doesn't mean he's not attracted to you, does it? I mean – I mean, Mummy said that lots of men were attracted to your type of person!'

Caroline swallowed convulsively. 'Your – your mother said that!'

'Yes.'

'But – but how? In what context?'

Laura shrugged. 'It was yesterday lunchtime. Before Daddy went sailing. She said that you were staying overnight in town.'

'And?'

'Well, she said you were probably staying with some man. She said you'd been living with some man before you came to Maitlands. She – she had the address.'

'Oh, *God*!' Caroline felt sick. So that was why James ... 'But why should she say a thing like that?' she asked bitterly. 'What's it to her?'

'You don't know Mummy very well, Miss Douglas. She likes talking about things like that. Not that she's interested in – well, in sex herself. Ever since the accident, she can hardly bear for Daddy to touch her.'

'You can't know that.'

'Oh, I do. She sort of – flinches, when he comes near. But that doesn't mean she doesn't care what he does. If ever any of the women who come here to dinner start flirting with him, she gets absolutely furious. She's very jealous, you know.'

'Laura, I don't think you should be talking about your mother like this.'

'Why not? You asked me about her.'

'I know, but—'

'Well! Haven't you seen those statues down by the pool? They were Mummy's idea. Daddy hates them, and so do I. You should hear what my friends say if they come here to swim.'

'Oh, Laura!'

'Anyway, like I said, she sort of intimated that you—' The girl halted. 'She didn't even know about Johnny coming here, but somehow she made me feel that if he had ... Oh, you know what I'm trying to say.'

'I think so.'

Caroline was trying to absorb the implications of what Laura was telling her. There were some people who got a positive delight out of tormenting others. *But her own daughter!*

Twisting her hands together, she paced to the windows, staring out unseeingly. Surely the idea which had just occurred to her could have no basis in fact.

Deborah Booth could not have been responsible for summoning John Mooney to Maitlands, could she? And yet, of all of them, she would have had the best opportunity. And she would have known that only Caroline could be expected to be at the house. James's being there had not been part of her calculations.

Caroline found she was breathing rather quickly, but the callousness of what she was considering affected her like a body blow. Was it possible? And if so, what did Deborah hope to get out of it?

But that was no use. She was condemning the woman without a shred of evidence. She was allowing emotion to colour the issue. Nevertheless, Laura had put her on her guard, and for that she was grateful.

Laura cleared her throat, attracting Caroline's attention. 'Is something wrong, Miss Douglas? You wouldn't – I mean – well, you wouldn't feel you had to leave just because – because my mother takes too much interest in people's personal affairs, would you?'

Caroline turned then, feeling the weight of responsibility upon her. 'I – no, of course not, Laura.'

Laura looked relieved. 'And I won't meet Johnny on Friday. I'll try and get a message to him.'

Caroline nodded. 'Thank you.'

Laura managed a small smile. 'I'd better go and get ready for dinner. Mummy told me you're joining us.'

Caroline nodded again. How she wished she wasn't!

CHAPTER EIGHT

CAROLINE wore a simple black gown for dinner, securing her hair at her nape in a chignon. The gown was ankle-length, sleeveless, with a cowled neckline which framed her unusually pale features. Made of chiffon, it merely hinted at the contours of her body, and to her eyes she looked anonymous. She was unaware that her pallor accentuated the shadowy depths of her eyes, and that the simple gown was an ideal foil for her extreme fairness.

She could hear voices from the library as she descended the stairs, and her nerves tightened. If only she had not allowed Deborah to persuade her to join them. But then she had not known what kind of a week-end this would turn out to be.

The library door stood ajar, but even so she hesitated on the threshold. These people were not her kind of people, and she closed her eyes for a moment, summoning all her courage.

'Miss Douglas! Are you all right?'

She opened her eyes to find Clive Lester at her elbow. He had obviously been standing near the door and had noticed her hesitation.

'Oh, yes,' she acknowledged hastily, forcing a smile. 'I – I was just drumming up the courage to go in.'

'You don't need courage looking as you do,' remarked Clive smiling in return. He took her arm. 'Come along. I'll do the honours.'

The room seemed full of people, but they soon resolved themselves into the elder Booths, the young man who was Irene Frobisher's son, and Deborah. Seated in her wheelchair, she dominated the scene, elegant in a deep blue gown, cut low in front to display the magnificent sapphire necklace which encircled her slender throat. There was

107

no sign of either James or Laura, however, and Caroline could feel the tension inside her increasing.

'Ah, Miss Douglas!' Deborah had seen her, and Clive had, perforce, to lead Caroline towards their hostess's chair. 'You look – beautiful, doesn't she, Clive?'

There was such genuine admiration in Deborah's voice that Caroline felt ashamed for imagining that she might have made that phone call.

'I've just made the same observation,' Clive was replying, good-humouredly. 'I should compliment you on your choice of partners for me, Deborah.'

Deborah laughed. 'Do you know everyone, Miss Douglas? No, of course you don't. Let me introduce you to my mother-in-law. Oh, and Trevor, too.'

During the introductions, Caroline became aware that James had joined them. As she spoke to the elder Mrs. Booth, accepting a cocktail from the tray that Jenny was circulating with, assuring Laura's grandmother of the progress she was making, she heard him talking to his father, and her hands became moist, and a trickle of perspiration slid down her spine.

Trevor Frobisher was unexpectedly nice. Tall, and huskily built, he had spent the last two years working in a laboratory in South Africa. Deborah left them alone together, taking Clive off to see a seventeenth-century snuffbox she had just acquired, and when Caroline showed a polite curiosity about his work, he told her he was interested in biochemistry. He added that he eventually hoped to work in genetics, and with a little encouragement went on to explain how biochemistry overlapped into both biology and chemistry, and was in fact a comparatively new science. They were discussing the importance of heredity in determining physiological characteristics when Laura appeared.

She stood for a moment in the doorway, and had she been older Caroline would have sworn she was making an entrance. And in fact, she might well have been doing so.

It was the first time Caroline had seen her out of trousers, and in an ankle-length dress of floral cotton, her dark hair newly washed and like black silk about her shoulders, she looked very attractive.

She looked all round the room, seemingly uncaring of the attention she was arousing, and then saw Caroline and made her way towards her. It was only as she reached them that she looked at Caroline's companion, and her eyes widened disbelievingly.

'Trevor!' she exclaimed in amazement. 'It is Trevor, isn't it?'

The young man coloured slightly, and Caroline found herself watching Deborah Booth's expression. Laura's mother was leaning forward in her seat, obviously intent on the scene which was taking place.

'Hello, Laura.' Trevor grinned. 'Don't tell me I've changed as much as you have. Hell, before I went away you were still wearing a gym tunic!'

Laura giggled. 'I still do, sometimes.' She stood looking incredulously at him. 'But you're so big! I don't remember you being so tall – or so broad.' She coloured then, shifting her attention to Caroline. 'I'm sorry, Miss Douglas, but Trevor and I have known one another since we were kids together. He's four years older than me, of course, but I could still climb trees better than he could.'

There was a murmur of amusement from her grandparents, and as though she had just realized they could be overheard, Laura made an apologetic gesture and turned to speak to her relatives. Clive appeared beside Caroline as the Booths drew Trevor into their circle.

'Well,' he said, amusement gleaming in his eyes, 'I've done my duty for the evening. Now I can start enjoying myself.'

Caroline sipped her cocktail, only half listening to Clive's lazy compliments. James was standing beside his wife's chair, his head bent to listen to what she was saying to him. In his dark dinner jacket, the white ruffled shirt a distinct contrast to his tanned skin, he looked the successful business man he was, not at all like the tormented individual she had encountered that morning. She wondered what he was thinking, how he really felt – and whether the physical attraction he had for her could be turned off and on at will.

Dinner was served a few minutes later, and to her relief Caroline found herself seated between Mr. Booth and Clive Lester. James and Deborah occupied either end of the long dining table which was laid with silver cutlery and crystal glassware, two three-branched candelabra waiting to be lighted when twilight fell.

The meal was superb – fresh salmon, duckling basted in an orange sauce, a cheese soufflé that was so light it required no eating. Even Caroline managed to eat some of what was put before her, concentrating on what Robert Booth was saying to her, determinedly avoiding looking in James's direction.

The candles were lighted half-way through the meal, and their flickering flames illuminated the panelled dining room with obvious effect. They also cast concealing pools of shadow on the diners, allowing Caroline to relax somewhat in the knowledge that James could no longer observe her discomfort.

Across the table, Laura was chattering away happily with Trevor Frobisher. It was obvious that the two young people found plenty to talk about and watching them, Caroline guessed that for the moment Laura had forgotten all about John Mooney.

She shifted her attention to Deborah. She, too, looked well pleased with herself, and Caroline thought she could understand why. But if she thought that Laura could be so easily diverted, she might be in for a not-so-pleasant disappointment.

When dinner was over, coffee was served in the lounge. This was a room Caroline seldom entered. Her duties did not include joining the family in their apartments, thank goodness, and outside of the library, she spent little time downstairs. It was also the room where Deborah had interviewed her on her arrival, and was no more appealing now than it had been then. It was not a comfortable room, but no one could deny its elegance. Caroline thought, rather traitorously, that it had a lot in common with Deborah.

Robert Booth began asking Clive whether he had read the report of some firm's collapse in the *Sunday Times* that morning and Caroline, seated rather uneasily on the edge of a stiff-backed armchair, tried to take an interest in her surroundings. But she was very much aware of James dispensing liqueurs from a cabinet near the windows, and she was not altogether surprised when he approached her and asked what she would like to drink.

'Nothing, thank you,' she denied, indicating the coffee cup in her hands. 'This is fine.'

James nodded, his expression controlled, and looking up at him Caroline saw that the strain she had seen that morning had not entirely dispersed. This close, he had a haggard look which was at once repelling and appealing, and she quickly looked down again before he should glimpse the responsive emotion she felt.

She sensed rather than saw him walk away, and only then did she realize she had been holding her breath. But thankfully, Clive had finally managed to escape Robert Booth's interrogation, and he squatted on his haunches beside her chair, grinning irrepressibly.

'Hansford Textiles!' he muttered in an undertone. 'Why would I be interested in Hansford Textiles when I've got a beautiful woman to talk to?'

Caroline couldn't help smiling. 'You're very good for my ego, do you know that?'

'Why? Because the lord and master doesn't approve of you being here?'

Caroline found difficulty in controlling her colour.

111

'Wh – why do you say that?'

Clive shrugged. 'I don't know. Maybe it's me he doesn't approve of. I only know he's been giving us some killing looks this evening.'

'You're imagining it!'

'Am I? Perhaps so.' Clive's eyes held hers. 'Or is it that he's jealous, hmm?'

'You can't be serious!' Caroline was flushed now, but she couldn't help it.

'Oh, I am. Caroline – may I call you Caroline? – you don't know what those green eyes of yours can do to a man. Right now, I can think of nothing more desirable than waking up every morning and finding them beside me on the pillow.'

'Just my eyes?' Caroline tried to be flippant.

'No, not just your eyes,' Clive asserted softly. 'All of you. Every goddamn inch—'

'Can't you find a chair to sit on, Clive?'

James's voice separated them as successfully as any physical barrier falling between them could have done. Clive straightened, flexing his aching back muscles, but not before Caroline had seen his expression and known exactly what he was thinking.

'Always the perfect host, eh, James?' he remarked cynically.

'Hardly perfect,' James returned equably.

Clive fingered his moustache. 'Deborah tells me you've been sailing this week-end. Where did you go?'

Caroline held her breath, but James was unperturbed. 'I drove down to Southampton. Tom Middleham keeps his boat at Calshot.'

Clive nodded. 'Oh, you went to Tom's place. How is he these days? I haven't seen him for years.'

James looked down at the goblet of brandy he held in his hand. 'He's fine. As a matter of fact, he's just got back from a visit to his son's place in Ireland.'

Clive glanced down at Caroline then. 'Tom's son

breeds racehorses,' he said, by way of an explanation, and she gave a polite nod.

The whisper of Deborah's wheelchair across the carpet warned them of her approach, but Caroline was almost relieved. Although James and Clive were talking amicably enough, she could sense their unspoken antipathy, and she felt a strong sense of resentment towards her employer. What game was he playing? How dared he display such a proprietorial interest in her affairs? Didn't he care that others might notice? And after what he had said to her that morning ...

'Well, now, is everyone enjoying themselves?'

Deborah's cheerful interruption seemed quite spontaneous.

'What else could we say after that magnificent dinner you devised for us?' responded Clive gallantly. 'As always, Deborah, the perfect hostess.'

His eyes flickered sardonically towards James as he said this, and for an awful moment Caroline thought he would say something more, but he didn't. Deborah smiled with satisfaction, looking up affectionately at her husband.

'Clive says the sweetest things, doesn't he, darling?' Her gaze moved on to Caroline's vaguely apprehensive features. 'Don't you think so, Miss Douglas? I've noticed our errant bachelor has had plenty to say to you this evening.'

Caroline moved awkwardly. 'Mr—' She cleared her throat. 'Mr. Lester and I hardly know one another.'

'Ah, but Clive's not a man to let the grass grow under his feet,' Deborah declared mischievously. 'It's time he found himself a wife, isn't it, James? A man needs a woman.'

Glancing at James' set face, Caroline wondered at Deborah's lack of perception. Couldn't she see that she was not arousing the right response? Didn't she sense the tension here?

'Clive's not the marrying kind,' said James at last, his voice cool and controlled.

'You could be wrong,' retorted Clive, looking down at Caroline. 'Like Deborah says, it's time I began thinking seriously about settling down.'

'This is very sudden, isn't it?' James's eyes challenged the other man's.

'Well, you know how it is. One day it just – hits you.'

Caroline could stand no more of this. She got to her feet and gesturing towards the wall cabinet nearby, she said jerkily: 'Did you collect this jade, Mrs. Booth?'

Deborah's tongue appeared for a moment, running exploringly over her upper lip. Then she made a moue. 'I think we're embarrassing Miss Douglas, Clive. Oh dear, and I was enjoying myself.'

'So was I,' said Clive, but he was looking directly at her husband.

'Whatever turns you on,' remarked James quietly.

'What turns you on, James?'

'Can we put some records on, Daddy?'

Luckily, Clive's offensive was neutralized by Laura choosing that moment to interrupt them. Trevor was at her side, and she looked more animated than Caroline had ever seen her. Deborah on the other hand seemed to have burnt out her energy, and seemed none too pleased that James should acquiesce to his daughter's request, and walk away with the two young people.

Clive fumbled in his pocket for his cigarettes. 'Well, Deborah, perhaps it's time I was taking my leave.'

'Oh, no, not yet.' Deborah roused herself sufficiently to protest. She looked up at Caroline. 'What would Miss Douglas do if you left?'

'Actually, I'm feeling rather tired . . .' began Caroline uncomfortably, but Deborah wouldn't let her get away with that.

'Nonsense! Perhaps it's the atmosphere in here.' Deborah's lips twisted. 'It is rather – close. Clive, why don't you take Miss Douglas for a spin in your car?'

'Oh, no, really—'

Caroline's desperate denial was ignored, and Clive had brightened up considerably. 'Hey, Deborah, that's a good idea. You're sure you don't mind?'

'Why should I mind?' Deborah was looking very pleased with herself again. 'After all, this can't be much fun for you – two old marrried couples and a pair of teenagers. You go ahead, enjoy yourselves.'

Caroline could feel her nails digging into her palms. They were treating her like a schoolgirl being offered an unexpected outing. She was tempted to tell them that she had no desire to go riding with Clive Lester, that she was tired and she was going to bed.

But the memory of James's behaviour made her hesitate. If she did refuse to go out with him, what interpretation would Clive put on it? He was already suspicious of James's attitude towards her. Could she risk arousing a similar suspicion about her own feelings? She knew she could not, but she felt an impotent sense of frustration towards Deborah for putting her in this position. Why couldn't she mind her own business? Why should she care whether the governess was enjoying herself? Unwillingly, she remembered the things Laura had told her. But what was she getting out of this?

Clive slipped a hand under her elbow. 'Is that all right with you, Caroline?'

Caroline moved her shoulders helplessly. 'I – oh, yes. Yes, all right.'

Clive's smile was smug. 'Then you'd better get a wrap. My car's a convertible, and I rather fancy the idea of having the top down.'

Avoiding James's eyes, Caroline left the room. He was busy with Laura and Trevor, examining the records stacked in a cabinet below a perspex-covered hi-fi deck. Already the music of Simon and Garfunkel was flooding the room, and Caroline felt a pang remembering that she had once danced with James to that particular tune. Was he remembering it, too? And if so, what memories did it evoke for him?

'Where do you want to go?' asked Clive, negotiating the gates of Maitlands which Dodds had opened for them and turning out on to the Fenbourne road.

'Anywhere you like.' Caroline secured a chiffon scarf over her hair.

'That's very enthusiastic,' commented Clive dryly. 'I know you didn't want to come out with me, but really, I think it was the safest thing to do.'

'Wh – what?' Caroline was startled.

'You know what I mean,' returned Clive smoothly. '*James!* Didn't you notice the amount he'd been drinking? Another fifteen minutes and he wouldn't have given a damn what he said.'

Caroline caught her breath. 'I don't know what you mean.'

'Yes, you do. I'll admit, he got under my skin, too. But he does have a hell of life with that bitch, and I can't altogether blame him for being attracted to you.'

Caroline swallowed hard. 'Where are we going?'

'There you go, changing the subject again. What is it with you, Caroline? Surely you've got more sense than to get involved with your pupil's father!'

Caroline turned her head to stare out of the side windows of the car. 'Must we always talk about me? I could take you up on the things you said, you know.'

'What things?'

Caroline hesitated. 'Well – about wanting to settle down, for instance. That was a pretty obvious thing to say, wasn't it?'

Clive shrugged, glancing sideways at her. 'Perhaps I meant it.' Caroline made a disbelieving sound, and he went on: 'No, really. Deborah was right about that – a man does need a woman. And I've had my share of running around.'

Caroline grimaced into the darkness. 'And who did you have in mind?'

'That's a pretty obvious question, too, don't you think?'

'Me?' She gasped. 'Oh, honestly! I suppose you're going to tell me you fell madly in love with me at first sight!'

'Could be.'

'Oh, stop it!' They had reached the village now, and the lights from the Coach and Horses spilled out across the pavement. 'Where are we going?'

Clive slowed as a stray dog shot across the road in front of them. 'I suppose this place is as good as anywhere. Do you fancy a drink?'

'If you do.'

Clive made a face at her. 'Such enthusiasm! You'll turn my head!'

Caroline hid a smile. 'Could I do that, Mr. Lester?'

Clive helped her out. 'Very easily,' he told her solemnly, exposing her amusement. 'And the name's Clive.'

In fact, the next hour was one of the most pleasant Caroline had spent since coming back to England. Clive was an entertaining companion, and so long as they avoided personal issues, they got along very well together. He was interested in her work in Sri Lanka, and she found herself telling him of the poverty she had found there, and the austerity of life on a tea plantation. It wasn't until he was driving her back to Maitlands that he brought James's name into the conversation again.

'He'd never divorce her, you know,' he said suddenly, à propos of nothing at all, and Caroline stiffened. 'James, I mean,' he added. 'So there's no future—' He broke off. 'Do you know what I'm trying to say?'

'Yes.' Caroline looked down at her hands. There was no point in pretending. 'I only wonder why you think you have to say anything.'

Clive sighed. 'I like you, Caroline. I really do. In fact, I'd go further – I think I could quite easily fall in love with you.'

'Oh, Clive!'

'No, listen to me. I mean it. You're different from the girls I've known. For one thing, you work for a living. Most of the women I know would consider that a disaster! And you've travelled. You've seen something of life in other countries. You haven't just been content to sit at home and wait for some man to come along and make you an offer you couldn't refuse.'

Caroline's lips twitched. She wondered what Clive would say if she told him that had James been willing to marry her she would have been rapturously happy to do just that.

Instead, she made some deprecating sound, and he went on: 'I'm only speaking the truth. You're an unusual woman, Caroline, as well as a beautiful one. And I don't think you should be working at Maitlands!'

'It's nothing to do with you—'

'I know, I know. But I know James, Caroline. I know he's had one hell of a raw deal in his marriage. And I can't stand by and take the risk of his hurting you without—'

Caroline gasped. 'James Booth can't hurt me!'

'Are you sure about that?' Clive changed gear as the gates of Maitlands loomed ahead of them. 'If he doesn't, Deborah may.'

'Oh, for goodness' sake!' Caroline's fingers tortured a fold of chiffon. 'If you ask me, you're the one who's had too much to drink!'

Clive shrugged, sounding his horn for the gates to be opened, and then driving through. 'All right, perhaps I'm wrong.' He looked across at her. 'Can I see you again?'

'See me again . . .?'

'That's right. I'd like to take you to meet my mother. We could have dinner together.'

'Your mother?'

'Oh, yes, I have a mother. Believe it or not, I had two

parents.'

Caroline felt another smile tugging at her lips. But still she hesitated. She liked Clive, but she had no illusions about him. He was not a man she could fall in love with, even without ...

'Well, all right,' she agreed at last, realizing she was taking the easy way out. 'But I shall have to ask Mrs. Booth first.'

'She's not your keeper, is she?' Clive frowned.

'No, but ...' Caroline glanced up at the house as he brought the sports car to a halt at the foot of the steps. 'Can I ring you? Perhaps tomorrow?'

Clive nodded. 'Okay. The number's in the book. Double seven, double eight.'

'That's easy to remember.'

Clive turned, putting his arm along the back of her seat. 'Would you mind if I kissed you?'

'Do you usually ask?'

Clive shook his head, and bending his head explored her lips with his own. 'Mmm, nice,' he murmured, drawing back. 'Now, I suppose I'd better come in and say my good nights like the polite boy I am.'

Only Deborah and the in-laws still occupied the lounge, and Caroline expelled her breath with some relief.

'James is taking Trevor home,' replied Deborah in answer to Clive's query. 'Laura's gone with him.' She sounded tired now, and there were lines of strain etching her mouth.

'And we must be going, too,' exclaimed the elder Mrs. Booth. 'It's been a lovely party, Deborah.'

Good nights were not prolonged, and feeling rather *de trop* Caroline remained in the lounge while Deborah saw her guests to the door. But when the wheelchair sighed back into the room, she was ready to leave.

'Leaving me alone?' Deborah's lips twisted as Caroline moved towards the door. 'Don't you want to stay and say good night to my husband – and Laura, of course?'

Caroline felt the beginnings of a headache probing her temples. She thought it must be that which made Deborah's words sound so offensive. 'I – will you apologize to them for me, Mrs. Booth?' she asked politely. 'I do have rather a headache.'

'Really? And I thought you'd enjoyed yourself with Clive.'

'I did, I did. He's very nice.'

'Yes, isn't he?' Deborah's fingers suddenly gripped the arms of her chair tightly, almost as if she was in pain. But when Caroline made an instinctive move towards her, she relaxed, folding her hands together in her lap. 'Where did he take you?'

'Oh, just to the Coach and Horses in the village. We had a couple of drinks, that's all.'

'You took rather a long time over a couple of drinks.'

'I – we were talking. We didn't notice the time.'

Deborah regarded her closely. 'Oh, well, I suppose there are some things a girl needs to keep to herself.'

Caroline frowned. 'I don't know what you mean, Mrs. Booth.'

Deborah smiled then, but it was a rather unpleasant display of her teeth. 'I was not always confined to this wheelchair, Miss Douglas. I know what happens when a man and a woman are alone together – in a car.'

'I can assure you—' Caroline could not believe her ears. 'I hardly know the man!'

'All right, if that's the way you want it. In my day, we were not so coy!'

'I'm not being coy, Mrs. Booth.'

'And Clive didn't even kiss you good night, eh?'

'I didn't say that—'

Caroline was suddenly aware that they were no longer alone. She had not heard the car, but when she swung round, James was standing in the doorway, his face taut with contempt.

Caroline swung round again, staring at Deborah with

instinctive distaste. She had known James was there when she had asked her questions. But how long had he been standing there?

Caroline felt physically sick. 'I'm very tired, Mrs. Booth,' she managed to say jerkily, and turning, she walked deliberately towards the door. She did not look at James again, and he stepped aside at her approach. Without another word, she left them.

CHAPTER NINE

She had been determined that she was leaving when she went to bed, but in the morning, after a surprisingly good night's sleep, Caroline's determination had ebbed away. There was still Laura to consider, and the effect her abrupt departure might have on her. Maybe it was a foolish conceit, but she felt that Laura needed her perhaps more now than before.

Laura herself seemed in good spirits when they set to work in the library the next morning. She was still bemused by her reunion with Trevor Frobisher, and only when the telephone rang in the hall did a fleeting regret shadow her features.

'I haven't forgotten,' she said, looking suddenly depressed. 'I will write to Johnny – about Friday.'

Caroline gave a slight smile. 'You haven't forgotten about him, then.'

Laura's eyes widened indignantly. 'Because of Trevor? Of course not.' She hunched her shoulders. 'Oh, I know that's what Mummy hopes will happen, but she's wrong. Trevor and I – well, we're like brother and sister.'

'Are you?' Caroline shook her head. 'Well, don't let's get involved in an emotional argument. I'm not in the mood.'

'Did you have a good time last night? You made quite a hit with Clive, didn't you?' Laura persisted. 'You'd do well to cultivate him. He's an only son, and his mother positively dotes upon him. They live in this gorgeous Georgian house—'

'I know.' Caroline cut her short. 'Leave it, Laura. Now – can we discuss the lessons to be learned from the politics of the French revolution?'

It was a surprisingly uneventful week after the pressures of the week-end. Caroline, to her relief, saw nothing of James and next to nothing of his wife. One morning Deborah did join them for their break, but on that occasion she was not inclined to be talkative, and Caroline was grateful.

On Thursday morning, however, Clive telephoned. Caroline had put off telephoning him, but his reproachful disappointment made her make the effort to see Deborah and gain her permission to join him and his mother for dinner on Saturday evening. As she had expected, Deborah offered no objections, and Caroline stifled any sense of conscience she might have felt about James. She owed him no allegiance, and maybe her friendship with Clive would help to bring that home to him, too. As Clive had said, James would never divorce Deborah, she should know that better than anyone, and anything else was unthinkable.

Then on Friday afternoon, while Caroline was endeavouring to dry her hair in her bedroom, Jenny came to inform her that there was a telephone call for her.

'For me? Are you sure?'

Caroline frowned, winding a towel turban-wise round her head, wondering whether it was Clive ringing to cancel their arrangements. As she descended the stairs, hoping to encounter nobody in this state, it crossed her mind that it might be John Mooney. But she dismissed the idea without too much anxiety. Laura had assured her two days ago that the letter cancelling their arrangements was on its way, and therefore she was totally unprepared for the Irish brogue which sounded so much more pronounced over the phone.

'Is that you, Caroline?' he asked, with evident satisfaction. 'Now, aren't I the lucky one to have caught you?'

Caroline glanced uneasily round the hall, and finding she was alone, demanded angrily: 'What do you mean by telephoning here again?'

'Ah, is that any way to treat a friend?'

'You're not my friend, Mr. Mooney.'

'Sure and I thought I was.'

'Why are you phoning me, Mr. Mooney?'

'You're not giving me a chance to explain,' he protested.

'Laura promised me she'd written to you,' Caroline went on. 'Hasn't she?'

'Now why would Laura be penning a letter to me?'

'To tell you she can't see you tonight. You mean she hasn't written?'

'Ah, I didn't say that exactly.'

Caroline controlled her temper. 'Mr. Mooney, unless you have some very good reason for telephoning here, will you please get off the line!'

He tut-tutted irritatingly. 'Aren't you the impatient one? And here was I thinking we were having a nice chat.'

'Oh, please . . .' Caroline sighed. 'What do you want? Did Laura write to you or didn't she? She can't see you tonight. Apart from anything else, she's not dining at home.'

'Sure, and didn't the girl's letter arrive yesterday?' he assured her unhurriedly. 'It was you I wanted to speak to, Miss Douglas. I wondered if you'd spend the evening with me.'

'*What?*' Caroline's voice had risen, and she glanced apprehensively round the hall again to assure herself that her sudden exclamation had not attracted attention. 'Don't be absurd!'

'What's absurd? I'm here in Fenbourne already. It's my day off, you see. Why shouldn't I ask you to take pity on me and share my lonely dinner?'

'If you're lonely, Mr. Mooney, it's no concern of mine. And you had no right in coming here on the offchance that I might agree!'

'Why not? It's a free country, isn't it? I enjoyed the outing.'

Caroline shifted impatiently, feeling the ends of the towel coming down about her ears. 'Well – well, thank you for the invitation, but I'm afraid I'm otherwise engaged.'

'You're going out with someone else?'

Caroline raised her eyes heavenward. 'I have – other things to do.'

There was silence for so long that she half thought he had hung up on her. But presently he said: 'Is Laura there?'

So far as Caroline was aware, Laura was down at the pool. Trevor was spending the afternoon at the house, and later this evening the whole family were going to dine at the Frobishers'. How could she call her up to the house to speak to John Mooney? It did not bear thinking about. It would ruin Laura's evening, and her parents would be furious if they found out what was going on.

'I – you can't speak to her now,' she protested.

'Okay.' He was unperturbed. 'I'll ring later—'

'No! No, you can't.' Caroline was frustrated. 'Laura won't be here. I've told you, she's going out with her parents—'

'I'll take my chance.'

'Oh, *John*!' Caroline's fingers were gripping the receiver so tightly that it hurt. 'Oh – all right. What time do you want me to meet you?'

He was silent for another pregnant moment, and then he said softly: 'Are you mad at me?'

She sighed. 'What do you think?'

He sounded amused. 'I'm sorry. But there was no other way, was there?' He paused. 'Can you get down to the village? Or shall I fetch you?'

'No, I'll walk,' she answered firmly. 'Just tell me what time.'

'Well, let's say – seven o'clock, hmm? That will give us plenty of time to have a drink before dinner.'

Caroline hunched her shoulders. 'But not in Fenbourne.'

'Wherever you say. I'll look out for you at seven.'

'All right.'

Caroline replaced the receiver with a heavy heart. She was not at all convinced she was doing the right thing, but what else could she do? If she went to Deborah and told her the whole story, she would shed the burden, but not the responsibility. She had promised Laura to help her, and that did not entail causing more trouble between the girl and her parents. She had been hoping that the whole affair would eventually die a natural death, and John Mooney's attitude had encouraged that belief. What she had not bargained for was his transference of his attentions to her, or the complications that would bring. She was already in a nebulous position. Since the Irishman's visit to the house, both James and Laura were prepared to think that she had invited him, and this new complication would simply strengthen that belief. Somehow she had to convince John Mooney that he was wasting his time bothering with either her or Laura.

She had turned away from the phone, and was walking disconsolately towards the stairs, tugging the towel from her damp hair, when she realized that someone was watching her from the doorway to the library. It had to be James, she thought bitterly, her sense of guilt erupting into anger.

'Do you make a habit of listening to my conversations?' she demanded furiously, aware that she was venting her frustration on him. 'Is there no privacy in this house?'

James straightened from his indolent position against the door frame, his face revealing none of his real feelings. 'I'm sorry,' he said politely. 'But when I heard Laura's parents mentioned, curiosity got the better of me.'

Caroline twisted the towel between her fingers, her anger dispersing as quickly as it had come. 'You'll have gathered that it was John Mooney, then?'

A flicker of emotion crossed his face, but quickly disappeared. 'If you say so.'

Caroline halted, looking across at him, supremely conscious of the picture she must present in shabby jeans and a sleeveless shirt, her hair a damp weight about her shoulders. James on the other hand, was still dressed for the city, only the unfastened top button of his shirt, and his slightly loosened tie indicative that he was home for the day.

'Why do you think he was ringing me?' she asked at last.

James shrugged. 'I gathered he was making some arrangement with you. For this evening?'

He was coolly controlled, and Caroline could feel something inside her being squeezed, tightly. Holding up her head, she said: 'That's right, he was. Do you have any objection?'

James took a deep breath, and for a moment she thought he was going to denounce her, and then he pulled down his tie and turned away. 'Not at all,' he replied quietly. 'Now, if you'll excuse me, I have work to do.'

As he went back into the library and closed the door, Caroline had to steel herself not to rush after him and tell him what was happening. Perhaps he was the one person who might be prepared to help her. But for what purpose? And if he believed her, what interpretation would he put on her confiding in him? She dared not encourage him to believe that she still cared what he thought about her. Since that disturbing scene in the cemetery, too many similar scenes had returned to haunt her, and only by keeping out of his way could she hope to retain her self-respect.

As it happened, Caroline found no difficulty in reaching the village in time to meet John. When she came downstairs at about a quarter to seven, Groom was standing in the hall, and her initial anxiety that he was possibly waiting to take the family to the Frobishers' gave way under the realization that James would be driving himself.

'Going out, miss?' the chauffeur inquired politely, and Caroline nodded.

'Why, yes.'

'Can I give you a lift, then?' he suggested. 'I'm on my way to my sister's at Reading. If it's the village you're heading for, it's on my way.'

Caroline glanced about her. 'Were you waiting for me?' she exclaimed curiously.

Groom put on his peaked cap. 'No, miss,' he denied, but she was not convinced. 'Shall we go?'

Groom dropped her at the Coach and Horses, and climbing out of the sleek limousine Caroline saw the Irishman waiting across the street. Pressing her lips tightly together, she closed the car door, raising a hand in salute to Groom as he drove away. She had no doubt now that James had arranged for the chauffeur to take her to the village, and his concern for her safety was just another pain she would have to live with.

John Mooney came strolling across the road towards her, his smile not without a certain smugness. 'Well, aren't you an unusual girl? Early and all!'

Caroline looked irritably at him. 'I got a lift, as you saw.'

'Ah, I did that. A beautiful vehicle, wouldn't you say?'

'Oh, stop talking like that!' Caroline was in no mood for flippancy. 'Where are we eating?'

John surveyed her appearance appreciatively. In a brushed denim jeans suit, her hair secured in two bunches with elastic bands, she looked about eighteen, and he was not immune to her attractions.

'I've booked a table at the Phoenix – in Reading,' he told her, as they walked back across the road to where his motor-cycle was waiting. 'Are you hungry?'

'No. I just want to get this over with!' retorted Caroline, taking the helmet he offered her and securing it on her head. 'I'm ready.'

The Phoenix was a newly opened eating house near the city centre. Watching its clientele making their way inside as John parked the bike and stowed the helmets, Caroline realized that she was hardly dressed for such a place. But still, if he didn't like the way she looked, she didn't much care, and he at least was personable in his light grey lounge suit.

However, John was obviously approving of her appearance, and once they were inside and seated in the discreetly lighted bar, no one took the slightest bit of notice. He ordered Martinis, and after carrying them to their table, seated himself beside her on the low banquette.

'Cheers,' he said, and Caroline obediently sipped the dry vermouth. 'Now, what's wrong?'

Caroline glared at him. 'You ask me that! You know what's wrong. Blackmailing me into meeting you! I didn't know this was going to happen when I listened to you telling me what a realist you were!'

He shrugged, stirring his Martini with a cocktail stick. 'I never said I was a nice person,' he remarked lazily, concentrating on his task. Then he looked up. 'Why? What would you rather be doing? Having dinner with that attractive father of Laura's, hmm?'

Caroline had just taken a mouthful of her Martini, but John's casually spoken words made her choke and cough until the tears came to her eyes. So much for not being noticed, she thought, aware of several pairs of eyes upon them suddenly, as she wiped her mouth with a handkerchief.

'Bones in it?' he inquired softly. 'That's what my old lady used to say to me. Bones in it. I used to think that was very funny, her talking about there being bones in liquid.'

Caroline fought for breath. 'Why did you ask – what

you just asked?' she demanded.

He regarded the cherry on the cocktail stick for a moment, and then put it into his mouth rather thoughtfully. 'Well now, let me see, what did I say?'

'You know what you said,' she exclaimed in a low angry tone. 'Why did you say it? Has Laura – did she say something in her letter?'

'Would you like to be choosing your meal, sir?'

The waiter interrupted them, handing them each an enormous menu with the legendary bird that was fabled to rise again from its own ashes imprinted on the cover. John smiled and thanked the man, and then, realizing that Caroline was watching him tensely, he asked: 'Is it true?'

Caroline drew an unsteady breath. 'No, of course not.'

John consulted the menu in front of him. 'So – what are we going to have? I haven't eaten here before, so I can't recommend anything. How about trout? That sounds very nice. Or lobster? Do you feel like something fishy?'

'John, where did you get that information?' she pleaded, making no attempt to choose a meal. 'I want to know.'

He shrugged. 'What would you have me do? Play both ends against the middle?'

'I don't know what you're talking about.'

'I don't suppose you do. But I know and that's what matters. It's a temptation, I will admit.' He studied her anxious face mockingly. 'Oh, what's the point? You've said there's no truth in it, so what the hell!'

Caroline stared at him. 'Surely you can guess how I feel. John, you can't make a statement like that without elaborating upon it.'

'I can.' He frowned. 'Hey, what about steak? That's usually reliable—'

Caroline clenched her fists. 'John, unless you tell me what this is all about, I'll walk out of here right now, and no amount of inducement will bring me back!'

He sighed then, putting the menu aside. 'You won't like it,' he told her quietly.

Caroline stiffened, her thoughts racing confusedly. 'Have – have you been talking to James?' she burst out recklessly, and knew as soon as the words were uttered that he had not. But there was no way of withdrawing them now.

'James?' he queried, his eyes narrowed. 'That came out very – naturally, didn't it? That's Laura's father's name, isn't it?'

'Yes. Oh, yes, you must know it is.' She gripped the edge of the table very tightly.

'And is that what you call him?'

'No. That is – sometimes.' Caroline could feel her face burning in the semi-darkness. 'John, what is this—'

'What times?' he persisted, leaning back in his seat and she closed her eyes for a brief moment.

'I don't see what any of this has to do with you – or me – or Laura either, for that matter,' she cried.

'Do you make a habit of having affairs with married men?' he asked offensively, and she felt as though all the breath had been knocked out of her. She struggled to get up, a blind urge to get away from him possessing her to the exclusion of all else, but his hand on her arm was unexpectedly gentle. Holding her in her seat, he put his face close to hers. 'Who do you think told me?' he muttered, almost against his will. 'Only his *wife*!'

'What?' Caroline sank against the banquette, staring disbelievingly at him. 'But – but I thought – how do you know Mrs. Booth?'

'I don't,' he retorted, his mouth tugged down at the corners. 'I've spoken to her over the phone.'

'The phone?' Caroline tried to grasp this. 'Then you mean it was she who first called—'

'I don't know about that. I only know what she told me a couple of days ago.'

Caroline put her hand to her throat. There was too much to absorb here. It was inconceivable that Deborah should have been prepared to take into her house a woman she suspected of being involved with her husband. So how could she have discovered what happened between herself and James six years ago?

Turning to John, she said quietly: 'Exactly – what did she tell you?'

He stared down at the menu on the table in front of him. 'Why should I tell you? It's true, isn't it? I didn't believe it at first. That was why I was prepared to go along with her. But now ... I should never have said anything. Can't you forget I spoke?'

Caroline straightened her spine. 'But it's not true, John. Oh, I admit once James and I knew one another, but that was all over long ago.'

'*Knew* one another? Do you mean that in the biblical sense?'

'*No!*' Caroline was sickened. 'He's married, as you've pointed out. And contrary to common belief, I do not have affairs with married men. Or unmarried ones either, for that matter.'

'That's your story.'

'It's the truth!' She put a tentative hand on his arm. 'John, I thought you liked me ...'

'I did.' He glanced sideways at her. 'Now I'm not so sure.'

'Don't I even get a chance to defend myself?'

'What chance did you give his wife?'

Caroline bent her head. 'I'm not proud of what I did. My only excuse is that I thought – I thought James intended getting a divorce.'

'And he didn't?'

'No.' It was torture to talk about it like this. 'He only wanted a – an affair, as you say.'

'Well, I could say I'm sorry, but I'm not.' He shook his head. 'You deserve better than that, Caroline. Any man who was prepared to sacrifice your happiness to satisfy his own appetites isn't worth a second thought.' His hand closed over hers. 'Are we friends?'

'Tell me why Deborah rang you.'

'Have you chosen your meal, sir?'

In the silence that had followed Caroline's question, the waiter's voice came as an obvious relief to John. Flipping open the menu, he entered into a discussion with the man about the various dishes available, and Caroline waited impatiently for them to be alone again. She agreed to John's suggestion of steak and salad, with a seafood cocktail to begin with. In all honesty, she doubted her ability to swallow anything, but she would have agreed with anything for him to be gone.

As he walked away, however, John got to his feet. 'Let's have another drink,' he suggested, and Caroline couldn't prevent him from carrying their glasses to the bar.

At last he returned, and she appealed to him urgently: 'Why did Deborah ring you?'

'Did I say she rang me?' he countered after a moment.

Caroline's brows drew together. 'But – I thought you said—'

'I said I spoke to her a couple of days ago,' he corrected her smoothly, and she wished she didn't have the suspicion that he had worked that out at the bar.

Controlling her irritation, she went on: 'All right. Regardless of who rang whom, what was said?'

'What's the point of dragging all that up? Sufficient to say that the old girl was pretty cut up about your relationship with her husband!'

'Deborah's not an old girl! And what do you mean – cut up? And why would she tell you?'

John shrugged indifferently. 'Perhaps she hoped I'd take you off her hands.'

'What?'

'You heard. She must know if we're spending time together, you're not going to have much time to bother

133

about her husband.'

'But what does she know about James and me?'

He made a face. 'How should I know?'

Caroline wished she could believe him. 'And I suppose if you're involved with me there's less chance of you seeing Laura,' she countered bitterly.

'You could be right.' He leaned towards her. 'What does it matter? If she'd been going to sack you she'd have done it before now.'

Caroline quivered. That was not a reassuring thought. There was more to this than he was saying, and she wished she had not made the mistake of betraying her association with James. Until then, he had been prepared to dismiss Deborah's accusations as the imaginings of a frustrated woman. Now he was inclined to believe Deborah's story, whatever it had been.

Pressing her palms against the cool surface of the table, she said: 'How well do you think you know Deborah? What makes you think she's not just *using* you?'

'For what purpose?'

'I don't know.' Caroline felt helpless. 'She's an odd woman.'

'Is she?' John raised his eyebrows. 'In what way?'

'Why should I tell you?' Caroline made a futile gesture. 'Oh, I'll have to leave Maitlands. I can't go on like this.'

'What about Laura?'

Caroline hunched her shoulders. 'Yes – Laura. Poor Laura! What am I going to do about her?'

And James, a small voice was tormenting inside her.

John looked up as the waiter summoned them from the doorway. 'Come on,' he said, 'our table's ready. And I'm hungry.'

Caroline accompanied him into the lamplit dining room, with a heavy heart. What game was Deborah playing? Why should she tell a complete stranger that her husband had once been involved with her daughter's governess? It didn't make sense. If only John had been completely honest with her. The fact remained that Deborah had somehow learned of their past relationship yet she was still prepared to employ her! And for Laura's sake she ought to be grateful.

She was not surprised when John took every opportunity throughout the meal to talk of other things. So far as he was concerned, their conversation was over, finished. But what was he getting out of it? That was a question she could not ask.

Pushing her steak round her plate, she wondered if James was aware of his wife's knowledge. And if not, ought she to tell him? Heaven knew what Deborah was planning if she was telling men like John Mooney about her troubles. But why warn James? What had he ever done for her except complicate her life beyond all belief?

After the meal they had another drink in the bar, and now John returned to the subject which was uppermost in both their minds.

'You wouldn't really leave Maitlands, would you?' he asked softly. 'You wouldn't walk out on Laura like that?'

'What's it to you?' Caroline was bitter.

'I want to see you again.'

'You can't be serious!'

'Why not?' He looked hurt. 'It's not my fault if you get yourself into difficulties with your employers. And you must admit, I've been very understanding.'

Caroline could have laughed had it all not been so deadly serious. 'Understanding? You couldn't possibly begin to understand how I feel.'

He looked down into his drink. 'At least when I'm out with you, I'm not troubling Laura, am I?'

'Is that a threat?'

'Does it sound like one?'

'Oh, I don't know.' Caroline's head was beginning to ache. 'I suppose it's not your fault, as you say. I'm confused, that's all.'

He looked anxious. 'There's no need to be. Look,

maybe this Mrs. Booth just needed a shoulder to cry on. Mine was available, in a manner of speaking. You've still got your job. So far as you're concerned, everything's the same as usual.'

'Is it?' Caroline shook her head. 'I wish I could believe you.'

John insisted on running her back to the house, dropping her at the gates soon after ten. There was no sign of James's car as Caroline climbed quickly down from the motor-cycle.

'Thank you,' she said, handing back the helmet.

'Sure, it was nothing. Next week – same time, same place?'

Caroline caught her breath at his impudence. 'I may not be here next week,' she exclaimed.

'I think you will be,' he assured her, and she wondered what he knew and she didn't. He leaned towards her and touched her lips with his. 'Goodnight, Caroline. Sweet dreams!'

CHAPTER TEN

CAROLINE slept badly, waking several times in a cold sweat. Her dreams were punctuated by nightmare glimpses of Deborah, pursuing her relentlessly, the sound of the wheelchair whispering eerily round the room long after she was awake and trembling. She realized it was only the wind echoing through the eaves of the house, but that made it no less disturbing. Towards dawn she fell into a sound slumber from which Jenny awakened her with her breakfast tray.

Dragging herself out of bed, Caroline poured herself a cup of coffee, firmly convinced that she could not spend another night in this house. She was pale and haggard-eyed, and she was unutterably relieved that as it was Saturday she and Laura had no lessons that day.

She was still in her dressing-gown, drinking her second cup of coffee, when someone knocked at her door. Guessing who it might be, Caroline longed to be able to ignore the sound, but when Laura called: 'Miss Douglas! Are you there?' she knew she could not.

She opened the door and Laura came cheerfully into the room, her expression clouding somewhat when she saw Caroline's pale face.

'I say, are you all right?' she exclaimed, and Caroline knew then that so far as Laura was concerned everything was just the same.

'I'm fine,' she said determinedly. 'You're about early.'

Laura nodded. 'I just came to tell you Mummy wants to see you. She has something to ask you. Will you be long, do you suppose?'

Caroline sank down weakly on to the bed. 'I – well, I'm not dressed yet, as you can see.' She wished she felt more capable of dealing with Deborah, but after her disturbed night she felt drained of all strength. 'When – when does she want to see me?'

'Now. As soon as possible.' Laura was eager. 'Shall I tell her – fifteen minutes?'

Caroline was surprised at her urgency. Up to the present, she had not noticed Laura showing such regard for her mother's commands.

'You'd better make it thirty,' she conceded at last. 'If you'd like to go, I'll get my bath.'

Laura nodded smiling. 'Okay. See you later, then.' In the doorway she paused, however. 'By the way, I hope you'll agree,' she added confusingly, and left her.

Caroline bathed and then dressed in a salmon pink waistcoat-and-skirt suit, a chestnut brown shirt completing the ensemble. She was half tempted to start packing her belongings, but Laura's words had not been hostile, and she couldn't believe that Laura would want her to leave.

Deborah awaited her in the lounge. Mrs. French saw her coming down the stairs and gave her directions and Caroline walked more confidently than she felt into that elegant apartment. Seeing Deborah again was rather an unnerving experience after her nightmares about the woman, but she pushed such childish fantasies aside and said politely: 'You wanted to see me, Mrs. Booth?'

Deborah looked up from the newspaper she had been reading. 'Oh, Miss Douglas! Yes. Did Laura give you my message? Of course, she must have done or you wouldn't be here, would you?'

'Mrs. Booth—'

Caroline's instinctive desire to be honest with the woman was ignored as Deborah began speaking. 'I want to ask you a favour, Miss Douglas,' she said, her manner as friendly as ever. 'Laura needs some new clothes, and naturally, now that she's leading something of a social life, she wants to choose them herself. Unfortunately, I find the prospect of trailing round the London stores rather more than I can bear. I'm hoping to persuade you to go with her.'

'To – London?' murmured Caroline faintly.

'Yes. Groom would drive you, of course, and you could arrange to meet him later. Miss Douglas, you know London much better than I do, I'm sure. And you'll know the sort of thing Laura needs.'

Caroline badly wanted to sit down. Her legs felt distinctly unsteady, and a wave of faintness was making her feel weak. What was going on? How could Deborah tell anyone that her husband was involved with the governess and then ask that same governess to choose clothes for her daughter? Was somebody lying? Had John Mooney made the whole thing up? Was that the answer? Had it all been educated guessing on his part which had paid off? She had no way of knowing, and she stared helplessly at Deborah, wishing she knew what was going on behind that smooth façade she presented to the world.

'Is something wrong, Miss Douglas?' Deborah tilted her head curiously. 'As you're dining with the Lesters this evening I didn't think you'd have made any other plans.'

'I haven't.' Caroline got the words out with difficulty. 'Mrs. Booth—'

'Is it all fixed?'

Laura chose that moment to come sauntering into the room, hands pushed into the pockets of her inevitable jeans. Her mother looked suitably pained.

'I think it might be, Laura,' she told her daughter in a disapproving tone. 'I can't wait to see you in something other than those disreputable pants!'

Laura was looking at Caroline, noticing how pale she still was. 'Are you sure you're all right, Miss Douglas?' she exclaimed. 'If you're not well, we can go some other time . . .'

Deborah frowned. 'What's this? You didn't tell me you weren't feeling well, Miss Douglas.'

'I'm perfectly all right.' Caroline shook her head.

Mental confusion could not be termed a physical illness. 'Mrs. Booth, can I speak to you alone for a moment?'

Deborah folded her newspaper. 'Not now, I'm afraid, Miss Douglas. I – er – I have a lot of things to attend to. You go along with Laura, if you're sure you're up to it. I'll see that you're suitably remunerated for your time.'

Caroline stood for a moment longer, but Deborah's expression was unwaveringly adamant. Laura hovered by the door, impatient to be off, and Caroline knew that she could not say anything in the girl's hearing. With a helpless little shrug of her shoulders, she turned away, and as she did so James came to the doorway. In a cream corded suit and navy silk shirt, he looked lean and disturbingly masculine, the haggard look he always seemed to be wearing these days accentuating his dark attraction.

'Daddy!' Laura was delighted to see him. 'I thought you'd gone. Oh, are you going to give me a lift, after all? In the Jensen! Super!'

'Groom will take you, Laura.'

Deborah's voice had risen slightly, and it was obvious that she did not welcome this intrusion into her plans. But James was not intimidated.

'I told Laura I might take her up to town,' he stated levelly. 'As for bringing her back, Groom can drive up later this afternoon.'

'You're going to the office, James,' said Deborah sharply. 'You don't have time to run around after Laura.'

'Taking Laura up to town is hardly running around after her,' he remarked mildly. Then, to his daughter: 'Are you ready?'

Caroline glanced apprehensively from Deborah to Laura. What did this mean? That she was not going, after all? She half hoped so. She did not want to suffer the agony of spending an hour closely confined in James's car with him.

'I would prefer Laura to drive up with Groom,' insisted Deborah. 'Besides, Miss Douglas is accompanying Laura, and that car of yours isn't big enough for three.'

'The manufacturers wouldn't thank you for saying that,' he retorted dryly. 'And I did know that Miss Douglas was coming.' His eyes flickered coolly over Caroline. 'Are you ready, Miss Douglas?'

Caroline wanted to protest, but what could she say? She was only the governess. She turned helplessly to Deborah, and just for an instant glimpsed sudden hatred in the other woman's eyes. It was only for an instant, and she had no idea towards whom that hatred was directed, but it was sufficient to convince her that Deborah might well be capable of anything.

Her face suffused with colour and she turned back to James. He raised his eyebrows. 'I asked if you were ready, Miss Douglas,' he reminded her steadily. 'While I might not be quite as busy as my wife suggests, I don't have all day.'

Caroline's lips trembled, and she pressed them quickly together to disguise the fact. 'I – I'll get my handbag,' she said jerkily, and James stood aside to allow her to leave the room.

When Caroline came downstairs again, only Laura waited in the hall. 'Come on,' she exclaimed impatiently. 'Daddy's waiting!'

The Jensen was standing, with its engine idling, at the foot of the steps. Laura ran down the steps and swinging open the wide door, climbed into the back. By the time Caroline reached the car, James had left his seat and was standing waiting to close her door.

Caroline smoothed her skirt over her knees as the car purred down to the gates and Dodds emerged briefly to raise a hand in salute. Then they were out on to the Reading road, the Jensen gathering speed with little effort.

Laura sat forward, her elbows resting on the backs of their two seats. 'Isn't this super, Miss Douglas!' she exclaimed excitedly. 'I don't suppose you've ever been in a Jensen before, have you?'

'You shouldn't presume to make those kind of comments, Laura,' retorted James shortly. 'Miss Douglas is a lot older than you are. She's probably driven in Jensens dozens of times.'

Laura grimaced impudently. 'All right, all right. But she's not that much older. I was only making conversation.' She paused, and then went on: 'How much money can I spend, Daddy? Mummy says I need some dresses and things, but honestly, I need everything.'

Caroline wasn't listening to her. She was watching James's lean hands as they controlled the wheel. He had such nice hands, she had always thought so, brown, and long-fingered; hard hands, not like some of the men she had known.

'What do you think, Miss Douglas?'

Laura was speaking to her, and Caroline blinked. 'I'm sorry,' she exclaimed apologetically. 'What did you say?'

James glanced sideways at her, an intentness in his eyes which cut through the barriers she had raised between them. 'Laura was asking where you think she should start,' he told her evenly. 'Oxford – or Carnaby Street?'

Caroline dragged her gaze away from his and glanced over her shoulder into Laura's expectant face. 'I – well, I would suggest we start in Oxford Street,' she said. 'You want some formal clothes as well as casual ones. Most of the stores have teenage departments these days. You can get some attractive things in the most unlikely places. Carnaby Street's all right for way-out gear, but I don't think that's what your mother expects you to buy.'

'Couldn't you come with us, Daddy?' asked Laura hopefully. 'I wish you would—'

'Laura, I have a meeting in precisely forty-three minutes!'

'We can manage, Laura,' protested Caroline. James should not imagine she was a party to that suggestion.

Laura hunched her shoulders. 'Okay, okay. I just thought you might like to show some interest in your daughter for once.'

Caroline saw James hands tighten on the wheel. 'What is that supposed to mean?' he asked tautly.

Laura looked sulky. 'Well, you never spend any time with me any more. You're always attending meetings – or going sailing – anything to get out of the house!'

'*Laura!*'

'Well, it's true.' Laura's voice rose hysterically. 'You don't care about me, any more than Mummy does. It's true I used to think you did. You used to take me with you ...'

'Laura, you're embarrassing Miss Douglas!'

Laura sniffed. 'Why should I always have to beg for your attention? Just because Mummy's jealous of you taking me anywhere ...' Her voice broke, and Caroline stared blindly out of the window at the passing scenery, wishing herself anywhere than in this car at this moment.

The Jensen braked suddenly, and James pulled off the road on to the hard shoulder. He switched off the engine, and then turned in his seat to look at his daughter. What he saw made him utter an oath before pushing open his door and getting out to get into the back beside her.

Without a word, Caroline pushed open her door and got out, walking away from the car. Traffic zoomed swiftly by her, but she paid it no heed, looking across the ditches and thorny hedges into the fields beyond. James's relationship with his daughter was a private thing, between the two of them. She had no part of it – or of him for that matter. The pain was suddenly unbearable. It was useless trying to deny it any longer. She had never stopped loving him.

She found a narrow bridge across the ditch and a barred gate where she could rest her arms. The sun was strengthening its power, and the rays fell warm on her back. She had left her hair loose today, and the slight breeze from the passing cars blew strands across her mouth. She was wiping them away when James came to stand beside her. She looked at his weary face and then at the car parked several yards away, and would have moved towards it had his hand on her upper arm not prevented her. He had his back to the car, so Laura could not possibly see what he was doing.

'Don't go,' he muttered savagely. 'Not yet. Please – Caroline!'

Caroline quivered. 'What about your meeting?'

'To hell with the meeting!'

'You don't mean that. You have to go. You know you do.'

He sighed heavily, and nodded. 'I've promised Laura I'll take you to lunch. The meeting will be over by then ...'

'You don't have to take me,' protested Caroline at once. 'I'll go shopping with Laura, then I'll meet her later—'

'Don't be a fool!' he muttered huskily. 'Of course you're having lunch with us!'

'Poor Laura,' murmured Caroline, and he looked down at her, naked hunger burning in his eyes.

'Poor Laura indeed,' he agreed, between his teeth. 'A mother who never wanted her, who really doesn't care a damn about her – and a father who's in love with another woman!'

Caroline would have pulled away from him then, but he wouldn't let her go. 'It's true,' he said fiercely. 'I have to tell you. What's the point of denying it? But what can I do about it? Take Laura away, maybe? I've thought of that. But do you think Deborah would let me? Not on your life. And there's not a court in the land that would grant me custody of my daughter. Particularly not if there was any suspicion of another woman being involved. Okay, so Laura's sixteen, and in two years she'll be old enough to decide for herself. But can I wait that long? Can I take the chance that the woman I love won't have married someone else by then?'

He closed his eyes for a moment, and then went on: 'So

– I tell myself, I should leave. In two years Laura will be free to come to me. But I can't do that either. Can you imagine the poison Deborah could seep into her mind during those two years? Can you imagine her telling Laura how her father lusted after her governess?' He made an impotent gesture. 'Caroline, I'd put you out of my mind. Six years is a long time. I was sure you'd have married by now – had a family of your own. I had no right to ask you to wait six years ago, even if you'd been prepared to do so.'

'Oh, James!'

'For God's sake, Caroline, don't look at me like that. You don't know the torment you've put me through these past weeks. I don't know how much more I can stand.' His lips twisted bitterly. 'But I suppose you get a certain satisfaction out of parading your conquests before me!'

'James, you don't understand—'

'I understand that you're hurting me – for whatever reason,' he retorted harshly.

A sudden movement from the car attracted Caroline's attention, and she turned to him helplessly. 'James, Laura's coming. We can't talk now.'

'What more is there to say?' he demanded coldly, and turned away.

From the way Laura hung on his arm as they walked back to the car, Caroline guessed that he had made his peace with her at least. She was glad. After all, Laura was the one innocent person in all this. All the same, she wished she could have told him what John Mooney had said. It could not be dismissed, and sooner or later it would have to come out.

London was crowded, full of tourists as well as the usual Saturday shoppers. Because of the difficulties with one-way streets, James dropped them on the fringes of the main shopping areas, promising to meet them at one o'clock at a little French restaurant off Cavendish Square. Laura was in high spirits. She had got her own way for once, and Caroline was carried along on the wave of her enthusiasm.

Most of the larger stores had accounts in the Booth name, and those that didn't responded equally eagerly to the credit cards which Laura's father had given her. She swept through all the boutiques, buying all kinds of things, leaving everything to be delivered to Maitlands. It was the way to shop, Caroline had to admit, and she determinedly put her own troubles aside to share in Laura's almost childlike excitement.

With an unlimited budget at their disposal it was not difficult to find exactly what they wanted, and Caroline indulged a latent desire to be a designer. Laura's youth and extreme slenderness allied themselves to the fashions of the moment, and she looked just as good in frothy chiffon as she did in well cut Levis.

'Oh gosh, I'm not bad, am I?' she exclaimed, parading before Caroline and the admiring assistant in an ankle-length gown that shaded through purple and mauve to palest blue, and had a kind of capelike effect to the bodice which concealed the hollows of her throat. 'Honestly, I didn't know I could look like this!'

Caroline smiled. 'Don't get too conceited. They have to be paid for yet. Your father may refuse to sign the bill.'

Laura giggled. 'He won't,' she said confidently, swinging round once more. 'He said I can spend what I like. And I have.' She sighed happily. 'Yes, I'll take it. Oh, and do you have something in a sort of midnight blue? Yes, midnight blue. Long – and sort of clingy.'

'Laura!' Caroline stared at the girl. 'That wouldn't suit you at all!'

'I know. But it would suit you. And Daddy said I had to get you something for coming with me.'

'Oh, no . . .' Caroline shook her head, stopping the assistant when she would have walked away. 'Thank you all the same, but no. I can buy my own clothes.'

Laura looked distressed. 'Maybe I shouldn't have told

you,' she exclaimed disappointedly. 'I should just have bought something and not told you.'

Caroline shook her head. 'Now how could you do that? You're not my size. Besides, I don't need anything, honestly. Laura – darling, it was a lovely thought, but no!'

Laura looked less anxious. 'You're sure?'

'Positive. Now go and get dressed. It's – well, it's almost a quarter to one.'

'Is it?' Laura gasped. 'Hasn't the time flown? I think I'll wear that cream suit I just tried on for lunch, hmm? I could wear it to go home, and these people could send my shirt and jeans with the rest of the things, couldn't they?'

'I see no reason why not,' Caroline nodded agreeably, and the assistant went with Laura to help her to change.

As she waited, Caroline wandered round the department. It had been kind of James to suggest buying her something as well. It was the sort of thing he did – like getting Groom to run her to the village the night before. She frowned, putting a hand to her head as her own problems crowded her brain. What was she going to do about James? It was all very well for him to talk about waiting until Laura was eighteen, but would he wait that long? And if he chose to exert pressure on her, could she resist him? If he ever found out how she really felt about him ... She moved restlessly. She would have to make some decision before the end of the month. But parting from him again would be so painful!

La Sauterelle was a very exclusive little restaurant, and Laura looked infinitely smarter in the swinging pleated skirt and jacket she had chosen to wear. They arrived at a little after one to find that James had not yet arrived.

'Isn't that just typical!' exclaimed Laura, with good-natured impatience, as they were shown to the table her father had reserved. 'A girl should keep her escort waiting, not the other way around.'

'And you think you're an emancipated female!' countered Caroline teasingly, refusing to allow her depression to spoil Laura's day. 'Why shouldn't a man keep a girl waiting, if she wants to be treated as his equal?'

Laura considered this. 'I don't think I'm such an emancipated female, after all,' she said at last. 'I don't like being kept waiting. I'm hungry, and the food smells delicious, doesn't it?'

The door to the restaurant opened and several people came in as she was talking, and at the back Caroline glimpsed a tall dark man. 'I think your worries are over,' she said, trying to still the sudden racing of her own heart. 'I think your father's just come in.'

'He has?' Laura looked up delightedly. 'Oh gosh, he has, and look who's with him!'

Trevor Frobisher was following the older man across the room, threading their way between the tables. James's eyes flickered over Caroline, and then he raised his eyebrows at his daughter. 'Well, well. What's happened to the infant?'

Laura made a face at him. Then she smiled at Trevor. 'Hello. What are you doing here?'

'Believe it or not, Trevor came to the office,' her father told her dryly, sinking into the chair beside Caroline.

'To the office?' Laura was surprised. 'But why?'

'Your mother knew I was coming up to town today,' explained Trevor eagerly. 'She rang this morning and suggested that as your father was in town, too, we might meet for lunch.' He grinned. 'I didn't know he was meeting you, too.'

Caroline found James's eyes upon her, and looked down in confusion. Their message was simple – this was Deborah's way of checking up on him, of finding out where he had lunch and with whom. She wished she could tell him there might be some deeper significance, that Deborah might also be making sure that at no time were *they* alone together. But this time Deborah had defeated her objective. By bringing Trevor along, James had evened the numbers, and it was natural that she should be paired with him.

Across the table, Trevor was telling Laura about a car he had been to see that morning. Since returning from South Africa, he had no transport of his own, but he was considering various models. Caroline tried to concentrate on what he was saying, but it was difficult with James's thigh brushing hers, and his arm along the back of her seat behind her.

'You've had a successful morning?' James was asking softly, and she nodded her head vigorously.

'Very successful. Laura's bought some beautiful things, haven't you, Laura?'

Laura said: 'Oh! What? Oh, yes,' and returned her attention to Trevor, and James half smiled.

'Leave them alone and talk to me,' he advised, his warm breath fanning her cheek. 'I'm a fool, I know, but I want to know how you feel, even if you hate me.'

Caroline was horrified that the others might have heard what he said, but it was apparent that they hadn't, and James sighed.

'Relax,' he told her calmly. 'Can you hear what they're saying?'

Over the general buzz of noise in the restaurant it was impossible to hear every word without concentrating very hard, and right now, Laura was concentrating on Trevor.

Caroline shifted in her seat, her knee brushing his leg, which he moved closer to hers. 'I – I don't hate you, James,' she said at last in a low voice. 'But I can't go on living in your house. At the end of the month—'

'Would you like something to drink, sir?'

The wine waiter stood at James's elbow, and with a muffled oath, James turned to the man. But it was obvious that they knew one another very well, and after a brief discussion, he went away.

'What are you ordering, Daddy?' asked Laura, leaning across the table towards him. 'May I have a Martini?'

'No, you may not.' James was smiling but firm. 'I've

149

ordered you a glass of orange juice, and Pepe's special cocktail for us.'

Laura wrinkled her nose. 'Orange juice!' she said disgustedly. 'I have Martini at home sometimes.'

'But you're not at home now,' retorted James, leaning back in his chair. 'Cheer up, he's putting something with a bite into it.'

'Oh – what?' Laura was eager.

'Would you believe – lemon?' suggested James lazily, and Laura picked up a knife and pretended to threaten him with it.

The cocktails were delicious, dry and sharp, the ideal stimulant before the meal. Trevor let Laura taste his, and while they were engrossed with one another, James said: 'What are you going to do at the end of the month?'

Caroline played with the glass between her fingers. 'You must know I have to leave.'

'Because of me?'

Caroline looked up at him, and then, unable to sustain the look in his eyes, down again, quickly. 'Partly,' she admitted.

'Why?' He was constrained. 'What have I done to force you to leave? I've kept out of your way as much as possible. You're so good for Laura—' He broke off abruptly and raised his glass to his lips, and when he lowered it again, he had himself under control. 'What will you do?'

Caroline expelled her breath unsteadily. 'I don't know. Get another job, I suppose.'

'In England?'

'I don't know.'

James put down his empty glass. 'Will you let me see you sometimes?'

'*No!*'

Caroline's refusal attracted Laura's attention, and she frowned. 'What are you arguing about, Daddy? Why is Miss Douglas looking so upset? What have you been saying to her?'

James shrugged, summoning the waiter and ordering more cocktails. 'Miss Douglas and I don't see eye to eye about certain things,' he replied shortly. 'Well, shall we order the meal?'

It was impossible to indulge in private conversation while eating a lobster *bisque*, roast duckling cooked in cognac, and sweet sugared pancakes. They drank a dry white Burgundy with the meal, and that, with the cocktails Caroline had drunk earlier, combined to ease her tension. Their conversation veered through the merits of British cars compared to foreign ones to the latest play being produced in London, and Trevor kept them all amused with his account of a safari he had made in Kenya.

But at last the meal was over, and over coffee James suggested that if Trevor required a lift home, he could take him.

'Well, we've finished our shopping, Daddy!' exclaimed Laura, surprising Caroline, who had expected another session that afternoon. 'Could we all go home together?'

'Laura, your mother said she would send Groom up this afternoon,' Caroline began, but James interrupted her.

'I don't suppose any arrangement has been made yet,' he countered coolly. 'You're welcome to drive back with me if you like.'

'Thanks very much, sir.' Trevor was grateful for the offer.

'Good. That's settled, then,' said Laura happily.

'Well, I have to go back to the office to pick up some papers,' said James, signing the bill the waiter had brought to him. 'Do you want to hang on here or come back with me?'

'Couldn't we just saunter along and meet you in the Bayswater Road or something?' Laura asked, frowning. 'Is that all right with you, Trevor?'

Trevor nodded, but he was looking rather awkwardly at

Caroline, and she guessed he did not relish the idea of having a chaperon. Intercepting the boy's hesitation, James glanced Caroline's way. 'Would you like to come with me and see the offices of Booth Industries, Miss Douglas? Or would you prefer to stay with the infants?'

The way his suggestion was phrased and Laura's immediate: 'Oh, yes, you do that, Miss Douglas!' put Caroline in an unavoidable position. 'Very well,' she said, and she knew her voice was cool and annoyed.

'That's settled, then.' Laura allowed Trevor to pull back her chair. 'We'll see you later, Daddy. What time? Shall we say – three quarters of an hour?'

James rose, buttoning his jacket, tall and disturbingly attractive. 'That should be enough,' he agreed. 'We'll pick you up near Queensway. Look out for the car.'

Laura nodded, and after giving Caroline an apologetic grin she went off with Trevor. Outside the restaurant, James summoned a taxi, and once they were installed in the back and Caroline was sitting as far away from him as possible, she said: 'This was quite unnecessary, you know. I could have arranged to meet you later, too. I needn't have gone with them. Besides, I could have caught a train home. This is my day off.'

James made no reply, sitting indolently on the seat beside her, his hands resting on his thighs, and contrarily she felt mean. As usual, she was behaving like a cat, just because she resented the undoubted power he could exert over her was afraid that alone with him she would betray feelings which at present she had under control.

'James ...' She said his name tentatively, and he turned his head to look at her.

'It's all right, Caroline, don't be alarmed. I haven't brought you to Booths for the big seduction scene,' he said bleakly. 'I really do have some papers to collect. You can wait downstairs if you prefer.'

Caroline turned to stare broodingly out of the window. She ought to be telling him about Deborah, not behaving like an outraged virgin. But it was incredibly hard to think of any way to broach the subject without creating a worse situation.

The skyscraper building on the Embankment was an ugly thing of concrete and glass, but once inside its swing glass doors its air of clean-cut efficiency and elegant design erased that image. A marble-floored entrance hall gave on to a bed of high-speed lifts, and air-conditioning kept the temperature evenly balanced whatever the extremes of weather.

The commissionaire emerged from his office as they entered the building, his eyes flashing curiously over Caroline. Then he looked at James. 'Will you be staying long, sir? Or shall I fetch your car round now?'

James halted. 'I'll fetch it myself, thank you, Charles.' He looked at Caroline. 'Miss Douglas will wait here while I—'

'No! I mean, that's all right, Jam – Mr. Booth!' Caroline bit her lip. 'I – I'll come up with you.'

James barely acknowledged this, striding away towards the lifts so that Caroline had to run to keep up with him. He didn't speak to her all the way up the penthouse floor, and when the lift doors opened he strode off along the corridor with a speed that defeated her.

He waited for her to catch up with him before entering what appeared to be his secretary's office, and then opened an inner door that led into his own office. Caroline barely had time to notice the attractive appointments before James had closed the door and was pinning her against it with the weight of his body; his mouth seeking and finding hers.

'I've wanted to do this all lunchtime,' he groaned into her neck, and she could feel the muscles of his thighs stirring against her leg.

'You said this wouldn't happen,' she protested huskily, and the smile he gave was wry.

'It wouldn't have, if you hadn't come up here. But you

wanted it as much as me, didn't you?' His eyes darkened. 'Go on, say it – tell me you don't like me touching you like this!'

Caroline moved her head helplessly from side to side, and with an exclamation his mouth covered hers again, with increasing urgency. She felt his hands unbuttoning her waistcoat and presently it fell to the floor, to be joined a few moments later by his jacket.

'You don't know what you're doing,' she breathed, but she was unable to prevent her own hands from probing the fastening of his shirt and finding the hair-roughened skin beneath.

'Oh, I know, Caroline,' he groaned, his tongue stroking her ear. 'I'm doing something I should have done years ago, something irrevocable, something that when Deborah finds out will mean that we're through! And let her do her worst. I don't care any more.'

'James!' Caroline disentangled her leg from between his. 'James, you don't mean that.'

'Caroline, I love you. I love Laura, too, but God help me, I *need* you. More perhaps than she needs me.'

Caroline took a deep breath, and although it was agony to do it, she dragged herself away from him, walking to the middle of the floor, wrapping her loosened shirt across her throbbing breasts, hugging herself closely. With her back to him, she said: 'James – I love you. I never stopped loving you. I realized that some time ago. But—'

'Oh, *Caroline*!' She felt him behind her, could feel the heat of his body before he jerked her back against him, moulding her body into his. His mouth sought her nape, and his hands cupped her breasts possessively. 'You know what you're doing to me, don't you?' he muttered thickly. 'Don't tell me not to touch you, because I can't help myself. I *want* you, Caroline. Not like this, but somewhere all to myself. I want to sleep with you, and not get up for a week. Caroline, come away with me. I'll get a divorce, anything you want, only don't turn me away!'

His words were more intoxicating than alcohol, exploding in her head with an urgency that was almost irresistible. To spend the rest of her life with James was all she had ever wanted, but could she allow him to do what he suggested at the expense of his wife and daughter? She knew she could not. With a little groan, she pulled herself away from him again, buttoning her shirt with trembling fingers, concentrating on the task as if it were a matter of life and death.

'You can't do it, James,' she said unsteadily, unable to meet his eyes. 'I – I won't let you.'

'Why not?'

His strangled words brought her round to face him, and the sight of his tormented face, the sensual attraction of his disturbed body, were almost her undoing. Pressing her palms together, she said slowly: 'James, you told me this morning how Deborah would react if you left her, how she might poison Laura's mind against you. Whether you believe it or not, you would be bound to regret giving her that opportunity sooner or later. Right now – right now—'

'Right now I want you,' he muttered savagely. 'Don't tell me you don't feel the same!'

Caroline sighed. 'James, of course I want you. No—' This as he would have reached for her again. 'But – but right now, you're only thinking of the present, not the future. All right, suppose you leave Deborah, suppose she gives you a divorce, what is Laura going to think of you? We've waited so long, James. Can't we wait just a little bit longer?'

'Can you?'

She turned away from the sight of him. 'I – I'll have to, won't I?' she got out jerkily.

There was silence for several seconds, and then he said harshly: 'And if I refuse?' He paused. 'You won't come away with me?'

Caroline could feel the tears pricking at the backs of her eyes. Swinging round, she stared tremulously at him, lips quivering. 'Oh – oh, yes, *yes*!' Her voice was breaking. 'Yes, I'll come away with you, if that's what you really want. But we shouldn't – *we shouldn't*!'

James moved towards her then, his hands descending on her shoulders, drawing her towards him. 'Oh, Caroline,' he breathed, resting his forehead against hers. 'Thank you. Thank you for saying that. I thought I was going out of my head.'

'Wh – what are you going to do?' she faltered.

He gave a heavy sigh, and she knew that for the moment he had himself in control again. 'I – know you're right, about Laura. But asking me to wait another two years . . .' He shook his head. 'Where will you go if you leave my house? How will I see you?'

'I don't think we should.'

'What?' His eyes darkened. 'You're crazy! God, Caroline, Deborah need never know.'

'You said that before. But somehow she's found out.'

James frowned. 'What?'

'Deborah knows. About what happened between us six years ago.'

James lifted his head. 'Who told you that?'

Caroline hesitated. 'It was something John Mooney said, that's all.'

'Mooney?' James stared down at her. 'Last night, you mean?'

'Yes,' Caroline nodded.

'My God! And how did he know?' James chewed on his lower lip. 'Why did you go out with him last night?'

Caroline hesitated. 'Will you believe me if I tell you?'

James took her by the wrist and drew her after him across to his desk. He lounged into the comfortable leather armchair behind it, and pulled her on to his knees. 'That's better,' he said, his voice suddenly thickening again. 'Go on. Before I get interested in other things.'

'Well—' Caroline didn't know how to begin. 'Do you remember that day he came to the house – when I went off with him on his motor-bike?'

'Do I not?' James slid her shirt off the shoulder nearest to him, his mouth caressing.

'Oh, James, please!' she exclaimed, her pulses racing as he continued to kiss her. 'Let me tell you first.'

'Caroline, if Deborah knows about you and me, we don't have to wait, don't you see?'

'But it's not like that.' Caroline pulled her shirt straight, ignoring his protest. 'That afternoon John—'

'John?'

'Yes, John – he had received a telephone call, or so he said, reputedly from me, inviting him to Maitlands.'

'But you didn't ring him?'

'As if I would!'

James was serious for a minute. 'Deborah hinted to me that you had known Mooney before you came to work for us.'

'What?' Caroline gasped. 'But I hadn't.'

'Go on.'

She noticed he didn't say whether he believed her or not, but she had to continue. 'Well – we never found out who made that call, but I wanted to talk to him about Laura. I don't know, I had some crazy idea that he might talk to me. And he did. He assured me that he had no illusions that you would ever let him marry Laura. She – well, apparently she and some other girls had made all the running, and she'd taken it all more seriously than I think he had intended.'

James was staring broodingly into space at this point, and she looked at him a trifle anxiously. 'You do believe me, don't you? James, I swear to you, I never saw John Mooney until that afternoon he came to the house.'

James looked at her, enigmatically at first, but then, as he saw her concern, the guarded look left his eyes. 'I believe you,' he told her steadily. 'Is there more?'

She nodded. 'He rang the house after that, asking to speak to me. I don't know how many times he rang, or whether he spoke to anyone else, I suppose he must have done, but you came in when I was talking to him.'

'But why did you agree to go out with him? Don't tell me that was to talk about Laura.'

'No, it wasn't. James, I didn't know what to do. Laura was with Trevor – oh, my God! They'll be waiting for us!'

'Let them wait!' retorted James comfortably. 'Carry on.'

Caroline sighed. 'Well, that's about it. He threatened to ring again and ask for Laura if I didn't meet him. I knew if Laura found out, she would be upset, and quite honestly, I was afraid of what he might say to her about me!'

'So you met him.'

'In the village. We had dinner in Reading, at the Phoenix.'

'I'm not interested in where. What did he say?'

'He asked me whether I wouldn't rather be out with you.'

'Did he?' James raised his eyebrows. 'And what was your reply?'

'I denied it.' She looked indignant when he gave a mocking snort. 'What could I have said? That I would rather be out with my pupil's father?'

James shook his head. 'Okay. Then what?'

'I asked him why he should ask such a thing, and that was when he said that Deborah had told him.'

'The devil he did!' James looked perplexed. 'Aside from wondering how Deborah should have such information to give, why should she give it to him?'

'I don't know. I don't think he believed it at first, but then . . .' She hunched her shoulders. 'I used your name, and he became suspicious.'

James slid one hand under the weight of her hair, cupping her nape. 'Don't worry, love. It had to come out sooner or later.'

'I know. But if Deborah knows, why hasn't she said anything, or done anything? I mean, this morning she asked me to go shopping with Laura. It doesn't make sense.'

'Nothing Deborah does these days seems to,' remarked James dryly. 'Did Mooney say anything else?'

'No. I got the impression he wished he hadn't said as much as he did. It was all right telling me so long as there was no truth in it. But if there was ... I suppose he was afraid I might tell you.'

'Hmm.' James rested his head back against the soft leather upholstery. 'Quite a puzzle, isn't it? It's not like Deborah to know something like that and not use it. Unless she's changed. I know she hasn't been well lately. She's seen the specialist a couple of times. But when I ask her she denies feeling unwell, so what can I do?'

'Perhaps she's going to offer you a divorce,' suggested Caroline, but he shook his head.

'Somehow I don't think so. She told me this morning that she's making arrangements for us to go on a cruise in August – with the Frobishers.'

'Will Trevor be going?'

'Maybe.' James turned his face into her neck. 'But I won't be.'

'James, you may have to. For Laura's sake!'

'And what will you do?' he demanded huskily.

'Stay in London.'

'With Frankland?'

'Oh, James, I thought I told you about him. We're just friends. Colleagues, if you like. He's a teacher, too. You'd like him, James. He's nice.'

James's expression darkened, and there was desperation in the way he jerked her mouth to his, kissing her with a passionate abandonment that left her weak with longing for him, her body aching for a satisfaction only he could give. Then, with an oath, he pushed her roughly off his knees and got to his feet, buttoning his shirt and pushing it into the loosened waistband of his pants.

'James?' She stood watching him anxiously. 'James, is something wrong?'

'Everything's wrong, isn't it?' he demanded, his eyes bleak. 'Oh, fasten your shirt, Caroline. You're not going to let me make love to you here, and I can't stand much more of this without doing just that!' He reached for his jacket, tossing her waistcoat to her. 'But you're mine!' he added grimly. 'And if any other man—' He broke off. 'Don't underestimate me, Caroline. I don't intend to let you go a second time.'

Caroline slipped her arms into her waistcoat, dreading the words she had to say. 'James, you know I'm supposed to be having dinner with Clive Lester and his mother tonight.'

He was raking combing fingers through his hair as she spoke, and she saw the way he stopped what he was doing, his hand resting at the back of his neck. 'I didn't know that.'

Caroline sighed. 'James, he asked me. And – and at the time it seemed a good idea.'

'Why?'

'So – so you wouldn't imagine I was interested in you.' She rushed on miserably: 'James, Deborah threw us together. Short of being rude, there was no way . . .' She bent her head. 'I don't care about Clive Lester, James. I don't care about anyone but you.'

There was silence for a few moments, and then, reluctantly it seemed, he came towards her. When he was near enough, she looked up and with a little sob threw herself against him. His arms closed about her, and she felt him shudder as he buried his face in the silken curtain of her hair.

Caroline heard the voices in the corridor seconds before he did, and she tore herself away from him saying frantically: 'I think it's Laura – and Trevor.'

James scowled. 'Oh, God! What do they want?'

'What will they think?' Caroline protested, trying to smooth her hair into some semblance of order. Her face felt bare of any make-up, she checked anxiously that her shirt was not unfastened.

James regarded her through narrowed eyes, his mouth frankly sensual. 'They'll think the worst,' he told her levelly. 'You look guilty already. Calm down. I don't mind.'

'But I do,' she cried, resentful that he could look so coolly controlled when only seconds ago he had been fully aroused. 'James, isn't there another way out of here?'

'Use the bathroom,' he suggested, nodding towards a door she had not previously noticed. 'And stop worrying. I love you.'

Caroline had scarcely closed the bathroom door when she heard Laura and Trevor come into James's office.

'What have you been doing, Daddy?' she complained, without rancour. 'We waited at the station, as you said, and then we decided we might as well walk to meet you. We came down Sloane Street, just in case you'd already left, and then when we got here, Charles didn't want to let us come up.' She sighed. 'Where's Miss Douglas?'

'In the bathroom,' returned James dryly. 'We were just about to leave. Sorry to be so long, but I've been showing Miss Douglas around.'

Trevor said something about the view from James's windows, and Caroline hastily applied a lipstick to her bare mouth. She didn't stop to do more than run a comb through her hair, and she felt a little less anxious when she emerged.

'Hey, so there you are!' exclaimed Laura, surveying her curiously. 'You look flushed, Miss Douglas. Has my father been getting at you again?'

Caroline exchanged a look with James, and he walked lazily towards the door. 'Mind your own business, Laura,' he told her, as she passed him, on her way out. 'I'll take care of Miss Douglas.'

CHAPTER ELEVEN

CAROLINE could not enjoy her evening at the Lesters', even though Mrs. Lester was a charming woman. Her thoughts were obsessed with what might be going on at Maitlands, and she contributed little to the conversation throughout dinner.

Afterwards, they all adjourned to an attractive living room, the furnishings expensive but comfortable, with none of the formality to be found in Deborah's house. Clive put on some records and then joined Caroline on the couch, obviously well pleased with the impression she was making on his mother.

'Clive tells me you've been working in Sri Lanka, Miss Douglas?' Mrs. Lester said, handing the girl a cup of coffee. 'I imagine you found that vastly different from working at the Booths'.'

'Vastly,' agreed Caroline, stirring her coffee.

'But apparently you've made quite a success with Laura,' went on the older woman, adding cream and sugar to her son's cup. 'And she isn't the easiest girl to get to know.'

'I like Laura,' replied Caroline honestly. 'And she isn't at all difficult, when you get to know her.'

Mrs. Lester completed her task and settled back in her chair with her own coffee. 'What about your employers? Do you get along well with them?'

Caroline wished she could have avoided this kind of questioning, kindly though it might be. 'I – don't see a great deal of them.' That at least was true.

'Hmm.' Clive's mother frowned. 'Perhaps it's just as well. Deborah's not a happy woman, is she, Clive?'

'She's not a well woman, Mother.'

'I know that. Irene Frobisher once told me that she has

terrible pain with her spine. It was broken, you know. But after all, she had no one but herself to blame for the accident!'

'*Mother!*'

'Well, it's true. Why shouldn't Miss Douglas be told?'

'Oh, really, I—'

Caroline's protest went unheard as Mrs. Lester went on: 'That poor man! She blamed him, you know, for her fall. She was pregnant at the time, and she ought not to have been riding at all. But she was mad on horses, mad on them! And furious because she was going to have a baby.'

Caroline was horrified. Until then, the details of Deborah's accident had been denied to her. James had never talked about it, and she had always assumed it had been a terrible mistake.

'She almost lost the baby, you know. It was born prematurely, and for weeks it was touch and go. Not that she cared. She didn't even want to see the baby – or her husband.'

'Mother, that's enough!' Clive looked apologetically at Caroline. 'I'm afraid my mother has a soft spot for James. That's all old history.'

'She ruined their lives!' asserted Mrs. Lester determinedly. 'If they weren't ruined already. What kind of life is left to either of them? She's a vindictive woman, Clive, and if she can hurt James, she will. Why didn't she divorce him years ago? She doesn't love him. I doubt she ever did. She's selfish and possessive. She'll keep him tied to her as long as she can. If I'd been him, I'd have left her.'

'There was Laura,' put in Caroline impulsively, and then flushed as both Clive and his mother turned to look at her.

Mrs. Lester considered her young guest's expressive face for a moment, and then she nodded. 'Of course,' she said. 'Why didn't I think of that?'

Clive drove Caroline home soon after ten and she avoided any embrace by getting out of the car almost before it had completely stopped. Clive's expression was wry as he looked up at her from the shadows behind the wheel.

'You've made your point,' he said. 'I wasn't going to touch you.'

Caroline sighed. 'I'm sorry, Clive. I like you, but there's no point in pretending anything more than that.'

'It is James, isn't it?' Clive pressed his balled fist against the steering wheel. 'I guessed last week, but I hoped I wasn't right. Then tonight, when Mother was talking . . .' He looked at her again. 'You're the woman he knew, aren't you? Five or six years ago. I knew there was someone, but I never knew your name.'

Caroline gasped, her hands gripping the opened window of the nearside door. 'But how could you know? No one knew!'

'Don't be a fool, Caroline. James's father knew, and the Frobishers. James took you out on his boat, didn't he? David Frobisher was bound to find out. He's secretary of the Yacht Club.'

'Oh, no!' Caroline pressed a hand to her mouth. 'What fools we were to think we could keep our relationship to ourselves!'

'What does it matter?' Clive's tone was flat. 'No one blamed James, least of all his friends. As I once told you, Deborah's a bitch!'

'She's his wife,' said Caroline bitterly, and turned away.

On Sunday afternoon Deborah sent for Caroline.

She had spent most of the morning in bed, dreading getting up, dreading having to face the fact that her days at Maitlands were almost over. It didn't matter now that she had seen little of James while she was here. He had been in the house, had slept beneath the same roof,

164

and she now acknowledged how much that had meant to her. To consider leaving, to consider denying herself the right to see him for another two years was an agonising decision to make, but somehow she had to find the strength to do it. Nevertheless, when Deborah sent for her, composure deserted her.

Her employer awaited her on the patio at the back of the house. Crazy paving stones were set with tubs of geraniums and hydrangeas, and a creamy pink clematis climbed over a wrought iron trellis. Deborah was sitting in her chair beneath a canopy of striped canvas, which matched the cushioned loungers positioned nearby. Beyond the lawns and rose garden Caroline could hear the sound of splashing and laughter from the pool, and she stiffened when Deborah said: 'This weather is ideal for outdoor swimming, don't you think, Miss Douglas? Laura's playing with her father. They're like children together. But then James loves the water. Swimming – and sailing – do you swim, Miss Douglas?'

Caroline's hands were twisted together behind her back. 'Yes, Mrs. Booth,' she answered politely, 'I swim.'

'I thought you probably did. Tell me, do you have a bikini, or do you go in for the more conventional type of swimwear?'

'I have a bikini. Mrs. Booth—'

'Yes, I expect you suit one.' Deborah's eyes narrowed as they took in the younger girl's slim figure. 'I never liked swimming myself. I preferred horse riding. Do you ride, Miss Douglas?'

'I'm afraid not.' Caroline's nails dug into her palms. 'You wanted to see me, Mrs. Booth?'

Deborah was looking towards the pool area. 'What do you think of my statuary, Miss Douglas? I suppose you've seen them down by the pool. Don't you think one of them looks rather like James – my husband?'

Caroline wished she could escape this awful cat-and-mouse conversation. She was convinced now that

Deborah was going to confront her with their relationship, and she wished she would get to the point.

'Mrs. Booth, what did you want me for?'

Deborah turned to look at the girl again. 'I want you to join us again for dinner this evening,' she said, her smile as deceptively genuine as ever. 'Since some of Laura's new clothes were delivered late yesterday afternoon, she wants an opportunity to show them off. Naturally, as you were with her, she wants you to see them, too.'

'Oh, really, Mrs. Booth, I—'

'You don't have any other plans for this evening, do you?' exclaimed Deborah impatiently.

'Not exactly, no. But—'

'Very well, then.'

'Mrs. Booth, I think we should discuss the termination of my—'

'Your probationary month with us, I know,' interrupted Deborah shortly. 'I realize there are only a few days left. And you don't want to stay on, do you?'

'I—' Caroline was nonplussed. 'No.'

'That's all right.' Deborah dismissed her. 'You can go, Miss Douglas. I promise you, we will talk later.'

And Caroline went – because she knew it was the only thing she could do.

Caroline wore the black velvet waistcoat and trousers she had worn on her first evening at Maitlands. Teamed with a cream lace blouse, the suit was plain but attractive, and she was aware she would need all her self-confidence this evening.

As she went down to dinner, she mentally rehearsed what her first words should be when she saw James. It was going to be terribly difficult behaving as if nothing momentous had happened, and she had the ominous feeling that Deborah was not about to let her get away with anything.

All three Booths awaited her in the library, and Laura's

very genuine concern that Caroline should approve of her appearance eased the slightly tense atmosphere. In an embroidered smock and long braided skirt, her hair looped above her ears, Laura looked tall and slim and mature, and it was no effort for Caroline to say something complimentary.

'Do I seem bigger?' exclaimed the girl laughingly. 'It's these sandals. Look!' She lifted her skirt to display thin high heels. 'They're terrifically good for my ego. I've always felt I was too small.'

Caroline forced a smile which included Deborah, and then James was beside her, asking her politely what she would like to drink.

'Oh, just something long and cool,' she said quickly, avoiding his eyes. 'Lemonade would be fine.'

James did not argue, and her eyes followed him as he crossed the room to the globe cabinet. He was not wearing a dinner suit this evening, but his bronze lounge suit was immaculate, fitting his lean body closely, accentuating the width of his shoulders, the powerful muscles of his legs.

Then realizing that Deborah was observing her, she said hastily: 'It's been a lovely day, hasn't it?'

'Trevor and I have been in the pool all afternoon,' put in Laura, and Caroline nodded.

'Your mother told me you and your father were enjoying yourselves,' she responded, and Laura frowned.

'Daddy wasn't with us.'

'You must have misunderstood me, Miss Douglas,' remarked Deborah coolly, and finding James's sombre gaze upon her Caroline did not contradict her. But she was sure she had not mistaken Deborah's words.

'Your lemonade.' James put the glass into her hand, and she thanked him automatically, wondering why Deborah got such pleasure out of baiting people.

It was a relief when Jenny came to say that dinner was served and they could all concentrate on the food. The lapses in the conversation were not so noticeable while they were eating. But half-way through the roast beef, Deborah decided to disrupt the uneasy calm.

'Miss Douglas tells me she wants to leave at the end of the week,' she said casually, helping herself to more horseradish sauce.

'What?' Laura reacted as Caroline was sure Deborah had hoped she would. The girl turned to her disbelievingly. 'Mummy's joking, isn't she? You don't really want to leave us, do you?'

'I—'

Before Caroline could say anything, Deborah broke in again: 'I'm not joking, Laura. Miss Douglas told me herself, this afternoon. Didn't you, Miss Douglas?'

'I—' Caroline was cornered and she knew it. But she had been hoping to break the news to Laura herself. Not brutally, like this. 'Well – yes,' she conceded. 'But—'

'Why?' That was Laura again, her young face flushed and distressed. 'I thought you liked it here. I thought we were getting on so well together. I thought we were *friends*!'

'We are, Laura!'

'I don't think Miss Douglas is any friend of yours, Laura,' remarked Deborah relentlessly. 'Or mine either, for that matter.' Her cold eyes challenged Caroline's, and she went cold, too. 'We employed her to be your governess, your companion – to help you to get over your infatuation for that man Mooney. Instead, Miss Douglas encourages the man to come here, speaks with him over the telephone, and what is more, goes out with him herself!' She ignored Laura's stricken expression and went on: 'I asked myself how she could have established such a relationship with him in such a short time. The answer was obvious – she had known him before she came here.'

'*No!*' Caroline was horrified. 'That's not true!'

She looked helplessly at James and was briefly reassured by the look in his eyes. 'You've got no proof of that, Deborah,' he said quietly.

'Miss Douglas only spoke to Johnny because I asked her to!' asserted Laura tremulously. 'She hasn't been out with him!'

'Really?' Deborah put down her knife and fork and bent to pick up her bag from the foot of her chair. She extracted a letter Caroline had never seen before and displayed it triumphantly. 'Then will someone tell me why he should be writing to her?'

Caroline gasped. 'But he hasn't—'

'Laura.' Deborah held the envelope so that the girl could read it. 'Is that or is it not Mooney's handwriting?'

Laura blinked and stared at Caroline's name written clearly in a scrawling hand. Then she swallowed convulsively. 'It – it looks like his handwriting,' she faltered.

'Let me see that!'

James snatched the envelope out of his wife's hand, and read it himself. Deborah watched him, a little smile playing round her mouth. Then she said smoothly: 'Why don't you read it, James? The letter, I mean. I have.'

Caroline's hands clenched on the edge of the table, as she stared at James's grim face. 'Yes, read it,' she burst out uncontrollably. 'Why don't you read it to all of us? Because I've never seen it before.'

'Haven't you?' Laura was pathetically eager to believe her.

'Ask Miss Douglas where she went on Friday evening,' said Deborah cruelly, and Laura glanced bitterly at her mother before looking at Caroline again.

'Oh, Laura! I did go out with John Mooney on Friday evening,' she exclaimed, and saw with a sense of loss how Laura's face changed at these words. 'But it wasn't like your mother's making out. It was all perfectly innocent—'

'Where did you get this letter, Deborah?' James spoke harshly. 'Have you been interfering with Caroline's possessions?'

Caroline saw the way Laura's eyes widened at her

father's casual use of her name, and would have said something more had Deborah not chosen that moment to explode her final bombshell.

'Why not?' she challenged coldly. 'Oh, poor Laura! Poor James! You've both been deceived, I fear.'

'Both?' Laura's eyes were tormented. 'What are you saying now, Mummy?'

'Laura, I think it's time you knew the truth. Miss Douglas – *Caroline,* as your father says – she and your father were lovers years ago—'

'No!' Laura's cry was piteous.

'—and no doubt he feels as distressed about her as you do about Mooney!'

'That's not true. We were never lovers!' Caroline pushed back her chair and got to her feet, staring despairingly at all of them. 'Whatever that letter says, I had no part of it. I've never seen it before, and you know it!'

'Why don't you read it, James?' asked Deborah again, and Caroline wrung her hands.

'You're evil!' she cried, as the other woman sat so calmly in her wheelchair, enjoying the chaos she had created. '*Evil!* You know there's no truth in anything you've said!'

'Daddy, were you and Miss Douglas – lovers?'

Laura's choked question was a desperate plea for reassurance, but James was in no mood to be reproved.

'What if we were?' he muttered savagely, turning the envelope over. 'What kind of a life do you think I have here?'

'Oh, *Daddy!*'

Laura thrust back her chair and rushed from the room, but when Caroline moved as if to follow her, Deborah's bony fingers fastened round her wrist.

'Leave her alone, Miss Douglas!' she commanded coldly. 'Don't you think you've caused enough havoc here? We have no further use for your services. You can pack and leave this house as soon as you like. The sooner, the better.'

Caroline dragged her wrist out of Deborah's grasp, feeling sick to her stomach. James still remained in his seat, fingering the letter, his lips twisted bitterly. He did not even look her way and she guessed that Deborah would have done her work well. Somehow she had persuaded John Mooney to write that letter, and Caroline's imagination could supply the damning words and phrases it would contain. James would read it, Deborah would see to that, and afterwards ... No doubt everything would go on as before, and she would have the added satisfaction of knowing that she had killed two birds with one stone. Laura was totally disillusioned about John Mooney, and would no doubt console herself with Trevor Frobisher, while James – James would no longer hanker after a woman he now held in contempt.

With a muffled sob, Caroline whirled and left the room, running up the stairs as if the devil himself was at her heels. It didn't take her long to pack, tumbling her belongings into her cases with an uncharacteristic disregard for their wellbeing. She didn't even bother to change. She put a poplin jacket about her shoulders and with a final look around, she went downstairs again.

To her astonishment, Groom was waiting in the hall. He took the suitcases from her unresisting fingers, and said: 'Mr. Booth said to drive you wherever you wanted to go.'

Caroline would have liked to have refused, but the idea of walking as far as the village with two cases defeated her. She followed Groom out to the car without a backward glance, and told him to take her to Reading station.

CHAPTER TWELVE

CAROLINE saw the notification that Deborah had collapsed and been taken to hospital in the newspaper three days later. It was a very small article, and she might not have noticed it at all had she not been scouring the papers looking for possible positions.

Since she had left Maitlands on Sunday evening, her brain had refused to function. She felt numb, making her way to Tim's flat with the instinctive reflexes of an injured animal seeking some place to lick its wounds. And Tim had been wonderful. After the way she had treated him, he could easily have turned her away, but instead he made her welcome, asking no questions except how long was she staying and would she be looking for another job? He had guessed her state of mind from her distressed appearance, and had shown her a gentleness and understanding which made her wish that she could have loved someone like him instead of a man who was not only married already, but willing to immediately believe the worst of her.

The news of Deborah's collapse was startling, bringing with it an aching awareness of her own uncertain future. What had precipitated such an event, and why had it happened? It made her feelings for James that much more poignant, and when Tim returned home that evening he found her in tears. He came into the flat, whistling, but when he saw her sobbing on the couch, he came and gathered her into his arms, cradling her like a child.

It was a relief to tell him at last. With stumbling honesty, she told him everything, from her own growing awareness of James to Deborah's cruel denunciation. She did not try to excuse her own culpability, she blamed herself for remaining at the house, for giving Deborah the opportunity to hurt both her husband and her daughter.

'But you still love him,' said Tim quietly, when her voice trailed away into silence. 'Don't you?'

Caroline sat up, drawing away from him, drying her eyes on the tissue he had handed her. 'There's no point, is there?' she asked, her voice betraying the veneer of control she was assuming.

'But you do?'

'Oh, yes. Yes. I suppose I always will!'

'Even though he was prepared to believe Deborah – knowing what she's like!'

Caroline drew a trembling breath. 'Deborah can be very persuasive. Besides, there was – the letter.'

'Oh, yes, the letter.' Tim got up from the couch. 'She must have paid him very well.'

'John Mooney?'

'Who else? You didn't know him, did you?'

'You know I didn't.'

Tim nodded. 'Well, I'm glad you've told me. You know I'll do anything I can to – well, to make you happy.'

Caroline nodded. Then she gasped. 'I forgot – there's an item in the paper. It says that Deborah's been taken into hospital.'

'What?' Tim took the newspaper she held out to him. 'What does this mean?'

'I don't know.' Caroline shrugged. 'She wasn't well. I think she had trouble with her spine.'

'Because of the accident. Of course. The spine is a very delicate mechanism.' He paused. 'I've been thinking – do you suppose she could have arranged the whole thing? You going to Maitlands, and so on? I mean – you said yourself you hadn't expected to get the job. There were others with more experience.'

Caroline looked up at him, lips parting. 'That's true. There were.' She swallowed convulsively. 'Oh, Tim, do you think she organized the whole thing?'

'Well, not Mooney, surely!'

173

'Why not? She could have done.' Caroline was trying to school her racing thoughts. 'But – to use Laura like that!' She looked up at him again. 'Could she have done something so – so vile?'

Tim shook his head. 'She sounds unscrupulous enough.'

'But to what end? To discredit me?'

'That – and to torment her husband.'

'Oh, God!' Caroline rose to her feet, twisting her hands together. 'I can't believe it.'

'Why not? What is it they say about hell having no fury?'

'But she doesn't love him!'

'No. But it's obvious she's a possessive woman. People have killed for less. Crimes of passion! You know it happens.'

'Oh, Tim, if that's true!'

'It sounds conceivable. She must have heard you were back in the country and set her little scheme in motion.'

'It – it's horrible!'

'But effective, you will admit.'

'And James – believed her!'

Tim walked into the kitchen and began filling the kettle at the tap. 'Honey, if I were you, I'd try and forget the whole thing. You're only going to prolong the agony by arguing the possibilities.'

'But I could tell James the truth...'

'Would he believe you? Why should he? He didn't before. And just suppose he did this time. Sooner or later he'd be bound to wonder about it. And you'd never know whether he really believed you, or wanted you in spite of it.'

'Oh, Tim! It's so – unfair!'

'Life often is,' said Tim philosophically. 'Look at me, keeping myself for a woman who doesn't even know I exist!'

During the following week, Caroline had three interviews. Two were at secondary schools in the London area, and the third was as governess to thirteen-year-old twins whose parents were going to spend a year in Africa. This latter position appealed to her purely from the point of view of getting away from England – and James. But Tim was not enthusiastic.

'You can't go running away, Caroline,' he told her quietly. 'You've got to come to terms with yourself. Booth is unattainable, and you've got to accept that.'

'I do. That's why I want to go away!' exclaimed Caroline.

'No,' Tim told her steadily. 'You're going away because you're afraid to see him again. Admit it! Caroline, stay in England. Face this thing. Marry me! I love you, you know I do. I could make you happy if you'd give me the chance.'

Caroline shook her head, knowing she was hurting him, but unable to prevent it. 'Tim, it's useless! I know what you say is true, but I'm a coward. I couldn't bear it if – I don't ever want to have to see him again. Can't you understand that?'

Tim nodded, his shoulders heavy. 'All right, Caroline, I won't say any more. A year's not such a long time. You might change your mind.'

Caroline smiled sadly. It was a vain hope after all these years.

The following week was filled with activities, shopping for a hotter climate, getting the necessary injections, checking travel arrangements with Miles Barstow, her new employer. Caroline was glad she had things to do. They kept her from thinking about James, from considering the thousands of miles she was about to put between them again. One afternoon she returned from shopping to find Tim in the flat, looking rather hot and flustered. But when she asked him what was wrong, he denied that anything was, and she assumed she had been mistaken.

The flight to Nairobi was leaving at eight o'clock on Friday morning, and on Thursday afternoon Caroline found herself on the Embankment, only a few yards from the Booth building. It was a crazy impulse which had brought her there on the eve of her departure, but in spite of all she had told Tim, she ached to see James, even from a distance.

As she strolled nearer, discouraged by the blankness of the windows, a black limousine pulled out of a side street and cruised to a halt outside the building. Two men got out of the limousine, also dressed in black, and Caroline realized with a feeling of trembling anticipation that one of them was James. Both men mounted the steps to the building as the limousine pulled away, James standing back to allow the other man to enter the swing door first. As he waited, he looked round, and across the stretch of the Embankment his eyes met Caroline's.

There was a moment when she stood transfixed, staring at him, and then with a gasp she turned away, hurrying back the way she had come. She heard him call her name, but ignored it, breaking into a run, but he had longer legs and was probably in better condition, she conceded, because he overtook her easily, grasping her arm and bringing her to a standstill. His action brought a few surprised stares from passers-by, but he seemed oblivious of them. He stared down at her as if he couldn't believe his eyes, and returning his stare she saw how pale and drawn he looked.

'Caroline!' he muttered, getting his breath back. 'God, he told me you were in Kenya!'

Caroline's lips worked soundlessly for a moment. Then she managed: 'Who?'

'Frankland. Your friend Tim Frankland! My God, I'll kill him!'

Caroline moved her head confusedly, hardly aware of the pain his fingers were inflicting on her arm. 'T – Tim?' she stammered. 'You've seen Tim?'

'Didn't he tell you?' James glared at her, and then shook his head incredulously. 'Oh, God, we can't talk here!'

Caroline partially came to her senses. 'There – there's nothing to talk about!'

'Damn you, isn't there?' He took several short breaths. 'Well, I say there is. Come with me.'

He strode off along the street, dragging her after him, and she stumbled to keep up. 'James – let me go!'

'No. You're coming with me. We're going to have this out, once and for all!'

'But – Deborah—'

'*Deborah!*' He halted abruptly, glaring down at her again. Then his eyes narrowed. 'You mean – you *don't* know?'

'Don't know what?'

'Deborah's dead, Caroline. She was buried yesterday.'

'Wh – what?' Caroline swayed, feeling suddenly faint. 'I – I didn't know.'

James stared at her for a few moments longer, almost as if he couldn't tear his eyes away from her, and then he strode on, still taking her with him.

'Wh – where are we going?' she protested.

'To the office. We can be alone there.'

'James, it makes no difference, you know!'

He halted again, and this time she ran into him, aware of the hard strength of his body against hers for a moment. 'What do you mean?' he demanded. 'Of course it makes a difference.'

The tall bulk of the Booth building towered beside them, and looking up at it, Caroline moved her head slowly from side to side. 'You – you didn't believe me,' she faltered, and he uttered a savage oath, startling Charles, the commissionaire, who had come to stand curiously at the entrance.

'What in hell are you talking about?' he muttered, shaking his head. 'Look, let's go inside. I don't enjoy making a scene where everyone can enjoy it!'

Caroline hung back. 'It's no use, James. I – I leave for Nairobi in the morning.'

'Like hell you do!' he retorted angrily, and swinging her slight body into his arms, he carried her past the astounded commissionaire and into the building.

There was a receptionist on duty at the desk in the foyer, and she looked wide-eyed at the spectacle of her boss's son carrying a strange young woman into the lift. But then the lift doors closed and Caroline and James were alone.

He looked down at her, struggling in his arms, and a strange expression crossed his face. Then he set her on her feet, and leaned back against the wall of the lift, arms folded, waiting for it to reach the top floor.

'You have no right bringing me in here!' she protested, smoothing down her skirt. 'What will your staff think?'

James ignored her, his mouth a thin cruel line in his unexpectedly pale face. The high-powered lift whined swiftly upwards, and within seconds the doors opened at the penthouse floor.

Taking her by the arm, James hustled her along the corridor towards his office. Remembering the last time she had been in the building, when there had been no sound of voices or the clatter of typewriters, as there was now, Caroline shivered. But she must not think of that, she told herself. She must remember that awful final evening at Maitlands, when James had held John Mooney's letter in his hands.

James's secretary looked up in surprise when they entered her office. 'Your father wants to see you, Mr. James,' she said, as he barely acknowledged her presence, intent on steering Caroline into his office.

'Ring him and tell him I'm busy for the moment,' he told her shortly. 'And on no account am I to be disturbed, do you understand?'

'Yes, Mr. James.'

The woman raised her eyebrows, and Caroline felt dreadful. What must these people be thinking of her – of either of them? She looked indignantly up at James, but he was opening his office door and did not return her scrutiny.

Once inside, however, Caroline pulled herself free of him, and hurried across to the windows, putting the width of the room between them. Whatever he said, she had to stand firm, and not be swayed by the disturbing magnetism he had for her.

James closed the door and leaned back against it. He seemed content for a few moments just to stand there and stare at her, and although his expression was grim, there were other emotions narrowing his eyes. He surveyed her intently, his gaze moving from her nervous face to the palpitating rise and fall of her breasts beneath the thin sweater, over her simple denim skirt to her bare legs and feet encased in thonged sandals. Then his eyes travelled up again, lingering on the trembling lips which betrayed her.

'What is this about going to Nairobi?' he asked at last, his voice taut with constraint.

'I – I've got a job. I – I'm going to work there.'

James straightened away from the door. 'So Frankland wasn't lying altogether. He'd just got the dates wrong.' His lips twisted. 'Or had he? Did you tell him to lie to me?'

'Tim?' Caroline frowned. 'No, of course not.'

'And he didn't tell you I'd been to the flat?'

'No.' Suddenly Caroline remembered that afternoon when she had arrived home and found Tim in such a state. 'I – I suppose he thought I – I wouldn't want to see you.'

'How paternal!' James was coldly sardonic.

'But why did you come to the flat?'

'Because Deborah had just died, and God help me, I needed you, Caroline.' James clenched his fists. 'Is that so incredible? I would have come for you sooner, but—'

'Come for me?' Caroline caught her breath.

'Yes, come for you.' James took a step towards her. 'Why do you sound so shocked? Was it all lies that you said to me here, in this room? When you told me you loved me? That you'd go away with me, if I asked you to?'

Caroline stared at him, the look in his eyes destroying all the defences she was trying to erect against him. 'I – oh, no,' she confessed weakly. 'You know it wasn't.'

'*Caroline!*'

With a groan he covered the remaining space between them, gathering her into his arms. His hard mouth found hers, and she knew she was crazy to imagine she could ever give him up. Whatever he had done, whatever he believed, he wanted her now, and common sense – a belief in what was right and what was wrong – meant little in the face of her feelings for him.

He was hungry for her, his mouth devouring hers, his kisses deep and passionate, his body straining against hers, making her overwhelmingly aware of their need of one another.

'James . . .' she breathed, when he freed her mouth for a moment, and he looked down at her with eyes glazed from his emotions.

'I love you,' he said unevenly, 'I love you. What more can I say? What more have I to do to prove it?'

Caroline found it difficult to speak coherently. 'But – but the letter,' she cried.

'Mooney's letter?' James frowned. 'What about it?'

'I—' Caroline bit her lip. 'Did – did you read it?'

'Yes, I read it. Why not? It didn't mean anything to you, did it?'

'James, I didn't even know there was a letter!'

'I know that. That's why I read it. I wanted to see how far Deborah had been prepared to go.'

'Deborah?' Caroline stared up at him. 'You mean – you

mean – you didn't believe her?'

James's eyes darkened. 'Did you suppose I might?'

Caroline felt a sob rising in her throat. 'Yes. Oh, *yes*! What else was I to think? You let me go...'

'Did you want to stay?' James absent-mindedly smoothed the damp hair back from her forehead. 'Caroline, let's get this straight first of all – you thought I accepted that story Deborah told about you knowing Mooney before you came to Maitlands?'

'I – yes.'

'But you'd already told me it wasn't true.'

'I know, but—' Tears trembled on Caroline's lashes. 'You sat there – you sat there with the letter in your hands.'

'I was stunned, I admit it. Stunned that Deborah should be prepared to go to such lengths...' He shook his head. 'Even then, I had no idea of the lengths she had already gone to. Unfortunately, she proved to be too clever for her own good.'

'What do you mean? How?'

James cupped her face in his hands. 'Do you love me?'

'Oh, you know I do.'

His mouth parted hers for a long disturbing moment, and then he lifted his head again. With a faint smile, he drew her across the room to his desk, sinking down into his chair and pulling her on to his knees as he had done once before. He kissed her again, more thoroughly this time, and then drew a deep breath.

'We have to talk,' he said huskily. 'I gather you knew nothing of Deborah's illness.'

'I saw that she had collapsed and been taken to hospital,' Caroline admitted quietly.

'But you didn't think to ring me and find out what was going on?'

'How could I? You know what *I* thought!'

James nodded. 'Of course. And I could tell you no different. After you left – and I was so glad you did; I didn't want you in that house after Deborah had revealed how unbalanced she could be — after you left — Laura ran away.'

'Oh, *no!*' Caroline sat up. 'Is she all right?'

'Now she is,' replied James quietly. 'But that night I was frantic for her safety. And to a lesser degree for yours. Why didn't you let Groom take you to your destination? He had orders to report to me after he returned to Maitlands, and all he could tell me was that you had asked to be taken to the station.'

Caroline shook her head. 'If I'd only known . . .'

'Well, anyway, I had Laura's disappearance to contend with, and ultimately Deborah's collapse.' He paused. 'She had a spinal growth. She had been in pain for weeks, the doctors said. But she refused to allow them to tell me.'

'Oh, *James!*'

'Yes. I think it was that which turned her mind. Oh, I guessed she'd found out about us from the Frobishers. Irene enjoys gossiping above all things. But I don't think she conceived her plans until she knew she was dying.'

Caroline stared at him helplessly. 'I — I'm so sorry.'

James shrugged his shoulders. 'So am I. But there was nothing I could have done. For some reason she decided she wanted to make me suffer, and you were the Judas sheep in her trap.'

'You know what she did now?'

'Oh, yes. I worked it out while she was in hospital, but after she was dead I went to see Mooney and heard the whole truth from him. It was all a set-up job to persuade me to allow Laura to leave Boscombe so that she could get you into the house.'

'But Laura caught pneumonia!'

'That was purely coincidental, the kind of luck Deborah had all the way along the line. Until the end. I could have strangled Mooney when he stood there and told me he'd done it all for money. And then afterwards I realized that to a man like him the promise of great rewards sounds very inviting. And after all, he had no real idea of the pain she would cause. I really think he liked Laura. He didn't want to hurt her. But once started along the path . . . Deborah forced him to continue.'

'And – and me?'

'Well, she knew you were an attractive girl. Irene had told her that. She guessed that Mooney wouldn't find it very difficult to transfer his attentions from an immature schoolgirl to a young and beautiful woman!' His lips twisted. 'If he'd touched you, I would have killed him. You believe that, don't you?' Caroline nodded, and he went on: 'That night after you left, we had a terrible row. She realized that I didn't believe her lies. And then Laura's disappearance – it was all too much for her. She collapsed the following morning when she was told that Laura had been found.'

'So – she did care about her daughter?'

'In her own way, perhaps. But she was quite prepared to use her to her own ends, and Laura's going to find it very hard to forgive her for that.'

'Where did Laura go?' Caroline asked.

'Not far. The police found her about five miles away, sleeping in a field. She was suffering from exposure and exhaustion, but unharmed.'

'Thank God for that!'

'I did, believe me. But then Deborah collapsed and was rushed into hospital, and for days I hardly left her side.'

'Oh, James!'

'She seemed to need me then. She hasn't needed anyone for years, but I think she regretted what she had done, if that's possible. At any rate, she died quite peacefully. I was with her.'

Caroline gulped. 'That was when you came to find me?'

'Yes. Does that sound terrible to you? It shouldn't. My pity for Deborah never altered my love for you.'

'James, I don't know what to say.'

'Say that you're not taking that job in Nairobi – say that you'll stay with me, and after a decent interval has elapsed, become my wife.'

Caroline pressed her lips tightly together. 'Oh, James! I want to marry you. I want to marry you more than anything else in the world!'

'Well?' he held her face between his hands. 'Why do you look so anxious?'

'I – Laura. Where's Laura?'

'Staying with her grandparents at the moment. Maitlands is going up for sale. I want to buy another house with more land attached. Does that appeal to you?'

She sighed. 'Oh, yes, yes. But, James – what about Laura?'

'She'll live with us, of course. If you have no objections.'

Caroline made a helpless gesture. 'Darling, I have no objections. But will Laura?'

'Ah, I see.' James caressed her lips with his thumb. 'You're worried about Laura accepting you.'

'That did upset her – about – you and me.'

'I know it. But Laura's growing up. She's almost a young woman. She realizes that a man needs – a wife. A real wife.'

Caroline hesitated. 'James, this job I'm supposed to be taking in Nairobi – why don't I take it?' She put her fingers over his lips as he would have protested. 'Wait – listen to me. Laura's had a traumatic experience. Don't you think it would be a good idea if you two had a holiday – together? Just the two of you. I could take this job for a couple of months, and then I wouldn't be letting the Barstows down either.'

'Caroline! Do you know what you're asking of me?'

'I know what I'm asking of myself, James.' She slipped her arms round his neck. 'Darling, don't think I want to leave you. Not now. But we're going to have so much ... Can't you see? If you have this time alone with Laura, it will be a turning point for all of us.'

James drew back to stare at her, his eyes disturbingly passionate. 'I just hope Laura appreciates what a stepmother she's going to have,' he said huskily. 'Caroline, I love you so much. If that's what you want – I'll do it. But afterwards ... We have so much time to make up ...'

A year later, a young woman cantered into the stable yard of a sprawling manor house, vaulted down from her horse, and tossed the reins to a grinning stable boy. Then she walked confidently up to the house, calling for Mrs. Evans, the housekeeper, as she entered the hall. Mrs. Evans appeared from the kitchen, wiping her hands on her apron. She was a small, rosy-cheeked woman, whose ample proportions did nothing to disguise her amiable disposition.

'They're coming, Mrs. Evans,' said the girl excitedly, and the housekeeper's face beamed.

'Oh, Miss Laura!' she exclaimed. 'Where did you see them?'

'I rode Jupiter up to the copse and I saw the car entering the park gates. Oh, Mrs. Evans, do I look all right?'

Mrs. Evans surveyed her young charge affectionately. 'Bless you, you look the picture of health. Put some weight on, too, I shouldn't wonder. You wait until your father sees you. He'll have no complaints.'

'I hope not.' Laura moved restlessly to the mullioned windows flanking the wide front doors. 'Oh, gosh, Mrs. Evans, here is the car!' She swung round anxiously. 'Is the champagne ready?'

The housekeeper smiled. 'You know it is. Go on with you. Open the door! They won't want to see me – not yet, anyway.'

Laura opened the door as Groom brought the Daimler to a halt outside, and she could see her father and Caroline in the back. Then her father swung the nearside door open, and climbed out, coming towards her smilingly.

'Oh, *Daddy*!'

Laura flung herself into his arms, noticing how well he was looking. She had grown accustomed to the lines of strain he sometimes wore, but now he looked years younger, his skin deeply tanned from the hot sun of Bermuda. Marriage to Caroline obviously agreed with him, and she forgave herself a momentary twinge of envy.

'How are you, love?' he asked, drawing back to look at her. 'Has Mrs. Evans been taking good care of you?'

Laura nodded vigorously, brushing away the foolish tears which had sprung to her eyes. 'I'm fine, Daddy,' she assured him, and then, with involuntary understanding, she turned to greet her stepmother, climbing rather self-consciously out of the back of the car. Caroline looked well, too, and apart from a slight nervousness, very happy. Laura went towards her.

'Welcome home – Caroline,' she said, and Caroline realized the girl was as nervous as she was.

'It's lovely to be home, Laura,' she said, and impulsively hugged the girl as her father had done.

She was touched by Laura's instantaneous reaction. With the same eagerness with which she had greeted her father, she returned Caroline's embrace, and foolishly Caroline found she was crying. Then, over Laura's head, she met James's whimsical smile, and she knew that everything was going to be all right.

At last, the author whose romances have sold more than 83 million copies has created her biggest and boldest bestseller...

Stormspell
ANNE MATHER

Ruth was young, she was innocent... until Dominic invaded her island home, and her heart...

Dominic was rich and powerful, bored and world-weary, fighting a temptation he had never before had to face.

Indigo was the island, Indigo: warm and colourful, and seductively romantic; drenched by the tropical sun and washed by the turquoise waters of the Caribbean...

And in the aftermath of the storm, it cast its own spell...

ONLY £1.50 from all bookshops

Published for the first time in Worldwide paperback, this blockbuster novel contains nearly 400 pages of enthralling, fascinating romance.

Anne Mather, author of so many bestselling romances, has really excelled herself this time – and at just £1.50 it's real reading value.

Look for 'Stormspell' at your local bookshop – it's available now.

WORLDWIDE

Best Seller Romances

Romances you have loved

Mills & Boon Best Seller Romances are the love stories that have proved particularly popular with our readers. They really are "back by popular demand." These are the other titles to look out for this month.

THE NIGHT OF THE COTILLION
by Janet Dailey

There was no denying the attraction that had flared up between Amanda Bennett and Jarod Colby from the moment they met – but he was rich and cynical, while she was poor and hadn't lost any of her ideals. How could she ever expect any happiness to result from falling in love with such a man?

THE SUN OF SUMMER
by Lilian Peake

On an enthralling holiday cruising down the Rhine, Marilyn couldn't be sure whether it was being made or marred by the attractive but mysterious Blair Barron. If only she could be sure how he really felt about her!

THE LOVE THEME
by Margaret Way

'I don't imagine the great Damian St. Clair will be thrown by a fashion plate – or will he? They say he's not unobservant of women,' declared Siri as she prepared for that all-important audition with the great conductor. How would she make out with the famous Damian as a singer – and as a woman?

Mills & Boon
the rose of romance

Best Seller Romances

Next month's best loved romances

Mills & Boon Best Seller Romances are the love stories that have proved particularly popular with our readers. These are the titles to look out for next month.

PRECIOUS WAIF
Anne Hampson

THE HOUSE OF STRANGE MUSIC
Margery Hilton

CHATEAU IN PROVENCE
Rachel Lindsay

DEVIL'S MOUNT
Anne Mather

Buy them from your usual paperback stockist, or write to: Mills & Boon Reader Service, P.O. Box 236, Thornton Rd, Croydon, Surrey CR9 3RU, England. Readers in South Africa-write to: Mills & Boon Reader Service of Southern Africa, Private Bag X3010, Randburg, 2125.

Mills & Boon
the rose of romance

FREE
information leaflet about the Mills & Boon Reader Service

It's very easy to subscribe to the Mills & Boon Reader Service. As a regular reader, you can enjoy a whole range of special benefits. Bargain offers. Big cash savings. Your own free Reader Service newsletter, packed with knitting patterns, recipes, competitions and exclusive book offers.

We send you the very latest titles each month, postage and packing free – no hidden extra charges. There's absolutely no commitment – you receive books for only as long as you want.

We'll gladly send you details. Simply send the coupon – or drop us a line for details about the Mills & Boon Reader Service Subscription Scheme.

Post to: Mills & Boon Reader Service, P.O. Box 236, Thornton Road, Croydon, Surrey CR9 3RU, England.

*Please note – READERS IN SOUTH AFRICA please write to: Mills & Boon Reader Service of Southern Africa, Private Bag X3010, Randburg 2125, S. Africa.

Mills & Boon

FREE Mills & Boon Reader Service Catalogue

The Mills & Boon Reader Service Catalogue lists all the romances that are currently in stock. So if there are any titles that you cannot obtain or have missed in the past, you can get the romances you want DELIVERED DIRECT to your home.

The Reader Service Catalogue is free. Send for it today and we'll send you your copy by return of post.

☐ Please send me details of the Mills & Boon Subscription Scheme.

☐ Please send me my free copy of the Reader Service Catalogue.

BLOCK LETTERS, PLEASE

NAME (Mrs/Miss) _____ EP2

ADDRESS _____

_____

COUNTY/COUNTRY _____ POST/ZIP CODE _____

the rose of romance

ROMANCE

Variety is the spice of romance

Each month, Mills & Boon publish new romances. New stories about people falling in love. A world of variety in romance — from the best writers in the romantic world. Choose from these titles in August.

JADE Sue Peters
IMPETUOUS MASQUERADE Anne Mather
DAUGHTER OF HASSAN Penny Jordan
PORTRAIT OF BETHANY Anne Weale
SEMI-DETACHED MARRIAGE Sally Wentworth
DINNER AT WYATT'S Victoria Gordon
ELUSIVE LOVER Carole Mortimer
HEARTLESS LOVE Patricia Lake
STAY TILL MORNING Lilian Peake
PRICE OF HAPPINESS Yvonne Whittal
HOSTILE ENGAGEMENT Jessica Steele
TOMORROW BEGAN YESTERDAY Sarah Holland

On sale where you buy paperbacks. If you require further information or have any difficulty obtaining them, write to: Mills & Boon Reader Service, PO Box 236, Thornton Road, Croydon, Surrey CR9 3RU, England.

Mills & Boon
the rose of romance